Echoes of Eternity:

THE TIME KEEPER

STEVEN LOWERY

The Time Keeper

For My Children,

May you go on endless adventures…

And For Ryan,

Thank you for all the adventures we had...

The Time Keeper

Chapter 1

The wind whispered through the ancient oaks, carrying with it the scent of damp earth and the distant promise of rain. Kaelen Mercer stood alone at the edge of the village cemetery, his boots sinking slightly into the soft ground. His gaze was fixed on a weathered gravestone, its surface worn smooth by years of wind and rain. The name *Elias Mercer* was etched into the stone, though time had begun to blur the edges of the   , as if trying to erase the memory of the man who lay beneath.

Kaelen's fingers traced the inscription, a habit he had formed over the years—a way of staying connected to the brother he had lost. Memories swirled in his mind, vivid and painful, as if they had only happened yesterday. He could still hear Elias's laughter echoing in the narrow corridors of ancient ruins, see the light in his eyes as they uncovered a long-lost artifact. Those were the days when life had been simple, driven by curiosity and the thrill of discovery. Those days were gone, shattered by a single, terrible moment that had left Kaelen with a wound that refused to heal.

He had always been the more cautious of the two, the one who would pause to consider the risks before diving into danger. Elias, on the other hand, had been fearless, his thirst for adventure never quenched. It was that fearlessness that had led them both into the depths of an ancient tomb on the day Elias died. Kaelen could still see the dark corridors stretching endlessly before them, feel the weight of the air growing heavier as they ventured deeper into the earth. He had warned Elias to be careful, to take it slow, but his brother had been so certain, so sure that they were on the brink of discovering something extraordinary.

The moment replayed in Kaelen's mind like a nightmare he could never escape. The sudden collapse of the ceiling, the sickening crunch of stone against flesh, the desperate scramble to pull Elias from the rubble. The look in Elias's eyes as he realized he wasn't going to make it, the way his hand had gone limp in Kaelen's grasp. It was a scene that haunted him, the guilt gnawing at him day and night.

"I'm sorry, Elias," Kaelen whispered, his voice hoarse with grief. "I should have been able to save you."

The guilt had become a constant companion, a heavy cloak that weighed him down no matter where he went or what he did. It haunted him in his dreams and followed him in his waking hours, a relentless reminder of his failure. Kaelen knelt beside the grave, placing a small, intricately carved stone at its base—a tradition they had started as children. Each stone represented a promise or a wish, a tangible symbol of the bond they had shared. This stone, however, was different. It was a vow, a silent pledge that Kaelen would find a way to change the past, to undo the moment that had torn his life apart.

"I've found something," he continued, his voice barely more than a murmur. "An artifact, a gauntlet... They say it can control time. I'm going to find it, Elias. I'm going to bring you back."

As if in response, the wind picked up, rustling the leaves overhead and sending a chill down Kaelen's spine. He stood slowly, feeling the cold seep into his bones. The village beyond the cemetery felt distant, almost foreign, as if it belonged to another world—a world where people lived simple lives, unburdened by the past. Kaelen knew he could never return to that world, not with the weight he carried.

He turned away from the grave, his mind already focused on the journey ahead. There was no turning back now. He had made his decision long ago—this was just the next step. The path he had chosen was dangerous, fraught with unknowns, but it was the only path that offered even the faintest hope of redemption.

The narrow cobblestone streets of the village were familiar underfoot, though each step felt heavier, more deliberate. The village, with its thatched roofs and smoke curling lazily from chimneys, was a picture of tranquility, but to Kaelen, it felt like a cage. He passed villagers going about their daily routines—shopkeepers opening their doors, children playing in the streets, women hanging laundry to dry—but their world seemed so far removed from his own. They greeted him with warm smiles and friendly nods, unaware of the storm raging inside him. Kaelen responded with curt nods and forced smiles, his mind elsewhere.

His thoughts drifted back to the day he had first learned of the Time Gauntlet. It had been a chance discovery, a scrap of ancient text buried deep within the private collection of a reclusive scholar in the capital. Kaelen had been searching for anything that might lead him to a way to undo the past, anything that might give him the power to save Elias. The text had been vague, filled with cryptic references and half-forgotten lore, but it had mentioned the gauntlet—a device said to be capable of bending time itself to the will of its bearer.

Kaelen had spent months tracking down every lead, every whisper of its existence, until finally, he had found what he was looking for. The knowledge had come at a price—favors called in; debts incurred—but it had been worth it. The Time Gauntlet was real, and it was within his reach.

As Kaelen walked through the village, he couldn't shake the feeling that he was being watched. The sensation was subtle, a prickling at the back of his neck that made him glance over his shoulder more than once. Each time, he saw nothing out of the ordinary—just the familiar faces of villagers going about their day. Still, the feeling persisted, gnawing at him like a distant memory trying to resurface.

He quickened his pace, eager to reach the village's historical archive. The building was tucked away in a quiet corner, its entrance marked by a faded sign that creaked in the breeze. It was a place Kaelen had frequented since he was a boy, a treasure trove of knowledge where he had spent countless hours poring over ancient texts and dusty tomes. The smell of aged parchment and the faint scent of dust greeted him as he pushed open the heavy wooden door, the familiar scents wrapping around him like a comforting blanket. The room was lined with shelves packed with scrolls and books, some so ancient they looked like they might crumble if touched too roughly.

A part of Kaelen had always found solace here, among the remnants of the past. The quiet stillness of the archive had a way of soothing his restless mind, offering a temporary escape from the grief that weighed so heavily on his heart. Today, even this place felt different—less a sanctuary and more a repository of the knowledge that had brought him to this fateful moment.

"Kaelen," a familiar voice called from across the room.

Alyssa stood near a table piled high with documents, her hair tied back in a loose braid. Her expression brightened when she saw him, though it quickly turned to one of concern as she noted the grim set of his jaw. Alyssa had known him for years, ever since they had first met during an excavation in the southern ruins. She had always been able to read him, to sense when something was weighing on his mind.

Alyssa's presence was a comfort, even if Kaelen hadn't always recognized it as such. She had been there when Elias had died, had seen the life drain from his brother's eyes, and she had stayed by Kaelen's side ever since. They had worked together on countless expeditions, uncovering secrets long buried by time, and she had always been the one to remind him that there was more to life than the past.

"You've been to the cemetery again," she said softly, her voice laced with understanding.

Kaelen nodded, offering a weak smile. "I found something, Alyssa. Something that might change everything."

He crossed the room, drawing a rolled-up parchment from his satchel. The weight of it in his hand felt significant, like he was holding the key to his future. Alyssa's eyes widened as she took the parchment from him, her fingers trembling slightly as she unrolled it. The room seemed to close in around them, the air thick with anticipation.

"An old text, hidden away in a private collection. It mentions a gauntlet, one said to have the power to control time," Kaelen explained, his voice hushed, as if speaking too loudly might break the spell.

Alyssa's brow furrowed as she scanned the faded script, her eyes narrowing as she tried to decipher the ancient language. She had always been better at this than Kaelen, her mind a finely tuned instrument for untangling the mysteries of the past.

"This… this is ancient, Kaelen. Where did you find this?" Alyssa asked, her voice filled with a mixture of awe and apprehension.

"An old collector in the capital owed me a favor," Kaelen replied, trying to keep his voice casual despite the excitement bubbling underneath. "He let me search through his private archives. Most of what he had was useless, but this… this could be it."

Alyssa continued reading, her fingers tracing the worn lines of text as if by doing so she could unravel its secrets. The more she read, the more her expression shifted from curiosity to concern. The words on the parchment spoke of a power that could bend the very fabric of reality, a power that had been lost to time for good reason.

"If this is real, if this gauntlet actually exists… Kaelen, you know what this means, don't you?" Alyssa's voice was barely above a whisper, but the weight of her words hung in the air like a heavy fog.

Kaelen nodded, his expression serious. "It means I might have a way to change the past. To bring Elias back."

Alyssa looked up at him, her eyes searching his for any sign of doubt, but she found none. The determination in his gaze was unshakable, a reflection of the resolve that had driven him to this point. Beneath that resolve, Alyssa saw something else fear. Fear of what he might find, fear of what might happen if he succeeded.

"Kaelen, we've been over this. Even if such a thing were possible, the risks—"

"I know the risks," Kaelen interrupted, his voice sharper than he intended. He took a breath, forcing himself to calm down. "I know, Alyssa. But I have to try. I can't just let things stay the way they are."

Alyssa sighed, setting the parchment down on the table. She reached out and placed a hand on his arm, her touch warm and grounding. "I understand why you want this but tampering with time… it could have consequences we can't even begin to imagine."

Kaelen looked away; his gaze fixed on the dusty shelves around them. The knowledge contained within those shelves had once seemed infinite, a boundless source of wonder and possibility. Now it felt like a prison, the answers he sought always just out of reach. "I've thought about nothing else for years. If there's even a chance—just a chance—that I can save him, I have to take it."

The silence that followed was heavy, filled with the weight of everything that could go wrong, everything they were risking. Alyssa was silent for a moment, her eyes softening as she watched him, sensing the desperation behind his resolve. She knew him too well to argue, knew that his mind was made up. That didn't stop her from worrying.

13

"You're going after it, aren't you?" Her voice was barely above a whisper, but it carried a strength that belied her concern.

Kaelen nodded. "I have to."

"Then I'm coming with you," she said firmly, leaving no room for argument. Her words were a declaration, a promise that she wouldn't let him face this alone.

He blinked, surprised by her determination. "Alyssa, you don't have to—"

"I'm coming with you," she repeated, stepping closer to him. "You're not going to do this alone."

Kaelen felt a wave of gratitude mixed with relief. He had expected her to argue, to try and talk him out of it, but instead, she was offering to stand by his side. It was more than he could have hoped for.

"Thank you," he said softly, the words inadequate to express the depth of his appreciation.

Alyssa gave him a small smile, though her eyes were still clouded with concern. "Just promise me one thing, Kaelen. Promise me you'll be careful."

"I promise," he replied, though even as he said it, he knew that keeping that promise might be harder than either of them anticipated.

The decision made; they spent the rest of the day preparing for the journey. Kaelen gathered supplies and weapons, checking and rechecking everything with meticulous care. Each item he packed felt like a piece of armor, a barrier between him and the unknown dangers that lay ahead. Meanwhile, Alyssa combed through the archives for any additional information about the gauntlet, her fingers flying over the brittle pages with a speed born of urgency.

By nightfall, they were ready to set out, the path ahead uncertain but the goal clear in Kaelen's mind. The village was quiet as they left, the streets deserted save for a few flickering lanterns that cast long, wavering shadows on the ground. As they walked, the weight of what they were about to undertake settled over them like a shroud, heavy and unavoidable.

As they reached the edge of the village, Kaelen couldn't help but glance back at the cemetery one last time. The gravestone was just visible in the distance, a silent reminder of why he was doing this. The wind whispered through the trees, carrying with it the faint scent of damp earth and the promise of rain.

He turned away, his resolve stronger than ever.

Whatever it took, whatever the cost, he would find the gauntlet. He would change the past.

And he would bring Elias back.

Chapter 2

The night was thick with the promise of rain, the sky above a canvas of swirling clouds that blotted out the stars. Kaelen and Alyssa moved quietly through the darkened streets of the village; their footsteps muffled by the damp earth. The air was heavy with the scent of wet leaves and wood smoke, a familiar smell that should have been comforting but instead felt ominous, as if the world itself knew of the dangerous path they were about to take.

Kaelen's mind was a storm of thoughts, each one crashing against the other as he tried to focus on the task at hand. The map he had carefully studied over the past few days was burned into his memory, each twist and turn, each hidden path leading them closer to the ancient temple where the gauntlet was said to rest. It was a journey fraught with danger, but it was the only chance he had to change the past.

Alyssa walked beside him; her face partially hidden by the hood of her cloak. She was quiet, but Kaelen knew her well enough to sense the tension in her posture, the way her fingers clenched around the strap of her satchel. She had always been the more cautious of the two of them, the one who thought things through before acting. It was a trait that had served them well on many occasions, and Kaelen was grateful to have her by his side now.

They reached the outskirts of the village, where the cobblestone streets gave way to dirt paths winding through fields and forests. The land here was old, ancient trees towering over them like silent sentinels, their branches twisted and gnarled from centuries of growth. The forest beyond was dense, a labyrinth of shadows and secrets that few dared to enter. But Kaelen knew the way. He had studied the maps, listened to the stories of the old men who gathered at the tavern, their voices hushed as they spoke of the cursed forest and the temple hidden within.

"Are you sure about this, Kaelen?" Alyssa's voice broke through his thoughts, soft but filled with concern. "There's still time to turn back. We could find another way."

Kaelen paused, turning to face her. The moon broke through the clouds for a moment, casting a pale light over her features. He could see the worry in her eyes, the doubt that lingered just beneath the surface. He also saw her determination, the strength that had always drawn him to her.

"I have to do this, Alyssa," he said quietly. "There's no other way. This is the only chance I have to bring Elias back."

Alyssa's gaze held his for a long moment before she nodded, her expression softening. "I know. And I'm with you. I just... I worry about what we might find out there. The stories..."

"I know the stories," Kaelen interrupted gently. "But they're just that—stories. We've faced worse before, haven't we?"

Alyssa smiled faintly, though it didn't reach her eyes. "I suppose we have. This feels different, Kaelen. This isn't just another expedition. This is—"

"Everything," Kaelen finished for her, his voice firm. "This is everything, Alyssa. I can't afford to hesitate now."

She didn't argue, but the worry in her eyes remained. Kaelen wished he could ease her fears, but he knew there was nothing he could say that would do that. The path they had chosen was dangerous, and there were no guarantees. It was a risk he had to take.

They continued in silence, the forest closing in around them as they left the village behind. The trees were tall and thick, their branches intertwining overhead to form a canopy that blocked out the moonlight. The darkness was oppressive, the only sound the rustling of leaves and the occasional snap of a twig underfoot.

Kaelen led the way, his hand resting on the hilt of the sword strapped to his side. He had always felt a sense of peace in the forest, a connection to the ancient trees that had stood watch over the land for centuries. But tonight, that peace was elusive, replaced by a sense of unease that settled over him like a shroud.

Alyssa stayed close, her hand resting lightly on the small dagger she carried at her waist. She was no stranger to danger, having faced more than her share of threats during their expeditions. This felt different, as if the forest itself was watching them, waiting for something.

The path they followed was narrow and overgrown, barely visible in the dim light. It wound through the forest, twisting and turning as it led them deeper into the shadows. The air grew colder, the trees pressing in on them from all sides.

"We should stop for the night," Alyssa suggested after what felt like hours of walking. "It's too dangerous to keep going in the dark."

Kaelen hesitated, glancing up at the sky. The clouds had thickened, obscuring the moon and stars entirely. The darkness was almost complete, the only light coming from the faint glow of their lanterns. He knew she was right—they wouldn't get far stumbling through the forest in the dark. Every moment they delayed was another moment lost, another moment closer to the possibility that he might never see Elias again.

He couldn't afford to push too hard. They needed to be at their best when they reached the temple, and that meant resting when they could.

"Alright," Kaelen agreed, though reluctance tinged his voice. "We'll rest for a few hours and continue at first light."

Alyssa nodded, relief evident in her expression. "There's a clearing just ahead. It should be a good spot to set up camp."

They continued down the path for a short distance before the trees began to thin, revealing a small clearing bathed in the faint light of their lanterns. The ground was covered in a thick layer of moss, soft and springy beneath their feet. It was a quiet place, the sounds of the forest muted as if they had stepped into another world entirely.

Kaelen set down his pack, glancing around the clearing with a practiced eye. It was well-sheltered, the trees forming a natural barrier against the wind. A good place to rest, but also a good place to be ambushed.

"I'll take the first watch," Kaelen offered, his hand still resting on the hilt of his sword. "You should get some rest."

Alyssa looked like she wanted to protest, but she nodded instead. "Alright. Wake me in a few hours."

Kaelen watched as she unrolled her bedroll and settled down on the soft moss, pulling her cloak tightly around her. It wasn't long before her breathing slowed, the tension easing from her body as she drifted off to sleep.

For a while, Kaelen stood guard at the edge of the clearing, his eyes scanning the shadows for any sign of movement. The forest was eerily quiet, the usual sounds of nocturnal creatures absent. It was as if the entire world was holding its breath, waiting for something to happen.

He found himself thinking back to the stories he had heard about this forest. Tales of travelers who had entered its depths and never returned, of strange lights that danced among the trees, luring the unwary to their doom. He had always dismissed those stories as nothing more than the superstitions of the old and fearful, but now, standing alone in the dark, he couldn't help but wonder if there was some truth to them after all.

His thoughts drifted to Elias, as they so often did. He could almost hear his brother's voice, teasing him for being so serious, so cautious. Elias had always been the daring one, the one who would charge headfirst into danger without a second thought. Kaelen had always been the one to hold him back, to remind him of the risks. On that fateful day, he hadn't been able to hold him back. And it had cost Elias his life.

The guilt weighed heavily on Kaelen's heart, a burden he had carried for so long it felt like a part of him. Now, for the first time, he felt a glimmer of hope. If he could find the gauntlet, if he could use its power to change the past, then maybe—just maybe—he could make things right.

Kaelen's grip tightened on the hilt of his sword. He wouldn't fail this time. He couldn't.

Hours passed in tense silence, the night growing colder as the temperature dropped. Kaelen's breath misted in the air as he kept watch, his senses alert for any sign of danger. Nothing came. The forest remained silent, as if it, too, was waiting.

Finally, as the first light of dawn began to filter through the trees, Kaelen turned back to the clearing. Alyssa was still asleep, her face peaceful in repose. He hated to wake her, but they couldn't afford to linger. They needed to reach the temple before nightfall.

He knelt beside her, placing a gentle hand on her shoulder. "Alyssa. It's time."

She stirred, blinking up at him with sleep-clouded eyes before she sat up, rubbing at her face. "Is it morning already?"

Kaelen nodded, glancing up at the sky. The sun was just beginning to rise, painting the horizon with streaks of pale gold and pink. "We need to keep moving if we want to reach the temple by tonight."

Alyssa stretched, rolling her shoulders to work out the stiffness. "Alright. Let's pack up and get going."

They worked in companionable silence, packing up their gear and ensuring that the clearing was left as undisturbed as possible. It was a habit they had developed during their years of expeditions, always careful to leave no trace of their presence behind.

As they set off again, the forest was gradually coming to life, the sounds of birdsong and rustling leaves breaking the stillness of the night. The path ahead was clearer now, the daylight filtering through the canopy and revealing the way forward. The sense of unease that had settled over Kaelen the night before had not left him. If anything, it had grown stronger.

They walked for hours, the forest around them becoming denser, the trees taller and more ancient with each passing mile. The air was thick with the scent of pine and damp earth, and the ground beneath their feet was soft with fallen leaves and moss. The path twisted and turned, leading them deeper into the heart of the forest, where the sunlight barely penetrated.

"This place feels… different," Alyssa remarked after a while, her voice hushed as if she were afraid to disturb the silence. "It's like we've stepped into another world."

Kaelen nodded, feeling the same sense of otherworldliness. The forest here was old, untouched by time, as if it had been forgotten by the rest of the world. The trees were enormous, their trunks thick and gnarled, their roots twisting through the earth like the bones of some ancient creature. The air was still, the sounds of the forest muted as if they were being swallowed by the dense undergrowth.

"It's not far now," Kaelen said, though he couldn't shake the feeling that they were being watched. He had felt it all night— the sense that something was out there, just beyond the edge of the light, waiting. Each time he looked, there was nothing.

They continued on in silence, their footsteps muffled by the thick carpet of leaves that covered the ground. The path grew narrower, the trees pressing in on them from all sides. It felt as if the forest itself was closing in, trying to swallow them whole.

After what felt like hours, they finally reached a clearing. This one was different from the one they had camped in the night before. The air here was thick with the scent of decay, the ground covered in a tangle of roots and dead leaves. At the center of the clearing stood a massive stone structure, half-buried in the earth and overgrown with vines. It was the temple.

Kaelen felt his heart skip a beat as he gazed at the ancient structure. It was just as the maps had described—a forgotten ruin hidden deep within the forest, untouched for centuries. The stone was weathered and cracked; the carvings that adorned its surface worn away by time. There was no mistaking what it was.

"This is it," Kaelen said, his voice barely more than a whisper. "This is where the gauntlet is hidden."

Alyssa stepped forward; her eyes wide as she took in the sight before her. "It's... incredible. How old do you think it is?"

"Hundreds of years, at least," Kaelen replied, his voice tinged with awe. "Maybe even older."

They stood there for a moment, taking in the sight of the ancient temple, its stones covered in moss and vines, its entrance dark and foreboding. It was a place that seemed to exist outside of time, forgotten by the world and left to decay in the depths of the forest.

Kaelen took a deep breath, his hand tightening around the hilt of his sword. "Are you ready?"

Alyssa nodded, though Kaelen could see the hesitation in her eyes. "As ready as I'll ever be."

They approached the temple cautiously, their footsteps careful as they navigated the tangle of roots and dead leaves that covered the ground. The entrance was partially blocked by a massive stone slab that had fallen from the structure, but there was enough space for them to squeeze through.

The air inside the temple was cold and stale, thick with the scent of mildew and decay. The light from their lanterns flickered on the stone walls, casting long shadows that seemed to dance in the darkness. The passage ahead was narrow and steep, the walls closing in on them as they descended deeper into the earth.

Kaelen's heart pounded in his chest as they made their way through the temple, the weight of the stone above them pressing down on him. The air grew colder with each step, the darkness more oppressive. It was as if they were descending into the very heart of the earth, where no light had ever reached.

They reached a chamber at the bottom of the passage, the air here colder and more stagnant than before. The walls were covered in ancient carvings, their surfaces worn smooth by time but still legible. The floor was littered with debris—broken stone, decayed wood, and the remnants of long-forgotten artifacts.

At the center of the chamber stood an altar, its surface covered in dust and cobwebs. And there, resting atop the altar, was the gauntlet.

Kaelen's breath caught in his throat as he approached the altar, his eyes fixed on the ancient artifact. The gauntlet was made of a dark, almost black metal, its surface etched with intricate patterns that seemed to shimmer in the light of their lanterns. It was both beautiful and terrifying, a relic from a time long past, imbued with a power that had been lost to the ages.

"This is it," Kaelen whispered, his voice trembling with a mixture of awe and fear. "This is what we've been searching for."

Alyssa stood beside him; her eyes wide as she gazed at the gauntlet. "It's… incredible. Kaelen, are you sure this is a good idea? We don't know what it's capable of. We don't know what could happen if you use it."

Kaelen reached out, his fingers hovering above the surface of the gauntlet. He could feel the power emanating from it, a pulse of energy that seemed to vibrate through the air. It was like nothing he had ever felt before—an ancient, primal force that called to him, beckoning him to take it, to wield it.

"I have to try, Alyssa," Kaelen said, his voice firm. "This is the only chance I have to bring Elias back. I can't walk away now."

Alyssa placed a hand on his arm, her grip firm but gentle. "I understand, Kaelen. But please, be careful. We don't know what we're dealing with here."

Kaelen nodded, his eyes never leaving the gauntlet. "I will."

He took a deep breath, steeling himself for what was to come. Then, with a steady hand, he reached out and grasped the gauntlet.

The moment his fingers touched the metal, a jolt of energy shot through him, his vision blurring as a wave of heat washed over him. He gasped, stumbling back as the gauntlet pulsed with a brilliant light, the patterns etched into its surface glowing with an intense, otherworldly energy.

"Kaelen!" Alyssa's voice was distant, barely audible over the roar of energy that filled his ears. He could feel the power of the gauntlet coursing through him, like a thousand lightning bolts striking his body at once. It was overwhelming, terrifying, and exhilarating all at the same time.

For a moment, he saw nothing except light, felt nothing but the searing heat of the gauntlet's power. Then, just as suddenly as it had begun, the light faded, the energy dissipating like smoke on the wind.

Kaelen collapsed to his knees, gasping for breath, the gauntlet still clutched in his hand. The chamber was silent, the air heavy with the scent of ozone. His body felt weak, trembling from the aftereffects of the gauntlet's power.

Alyssa was at his side in an instant, her hands gripping his shoulders as she helped him sit up. "Kaelen, are you alright?"

He nodded weakly, though his body still shook from the experience. "I... I'm fine. Just... give me a moment."

Alyssa's eyes were filled with worry as she examined him, but she said nothing, her grip on his shoulders firm. Kaelen could feel the lingering traces of the gauntlet's power coursing through his veins, like a distant echo that refused to fade.

"I've... I've never felt anything like that," Kaelen whispered, his voice hoarse. "The power... it's incredible."

Alyssa frowned, her concern deepening. "What did you see? What did it do?"

Kaelen shook his head, struggling to put the experience into words. "It was like... like I was being pulled in every direction at once. I could feel the past, the present, the future... all at the same time. It was overwhelming."

Alyssa's grip on his shoulders tightened. "Kaelen, this is dangerous. We don't know what this gauntlet is capable of. It could be more than you can manage."

Kaelen looked down at the gauntlet in his hand, the metal cool and smooth against his skin. The power he had felt was unlike anything he had ever experienced, but he knew one thing for certain—this was the key to changing the past. This was his only chance to bring Elias back.

"I have to do this, Alyssa," Kaelen said, his voice filled with resolve. "I have to try."

Alyssa's eyes softened, though the worry in her expression remained. "I know. But please, promise me you'll be careful. Don't let this power consume you."

Kaelen nodded, his gaze never leaving the gauntlet. "I promise."

With Alyssa's help, he got to his feet, still clutching the gauntlet in his hand. The chamber around them seemed darker now, the air thicker, as if the very walls were closing in on them.

"We should get out of here," Alyssa said, glancing around the chamber. "There's nothing else for us here."

Kaelen nodded in agreement, though his mind was still racing with the possibilities that the gauntlet presented. They made their way back up the narrow passage, the darkness pressing in on them from all sides. The air was colder now, the scent of decay stronger, as if the temple itself was trying to hold them back.

When they finally emerged into the daylight, Kaelen felt a weight lift from his shoulders. The forest around them was still and silent, the trees towering above them like ancient guardians. But the sense of unease that had settled over him had not lessened. If anything, it had grown stronger.

Alyssa glanced at him; her eyes filled with concern. "Kaelen, are you sure you're alright?"

He nodded, though his mind was still reeling from the experience in the temple. "I'm fine. We need to keep moving. We can't stay here."

Alyssa didn't argue, though Kaelen could see the doubt in her eyes. They set off through the forest once more, the gauntlet safely secured in Kaelen's pack. The sense of unease that had settled over him refused to fade, as if the power of the gauntlet had awakened something within him, something that he couldn't quite understand.

The forest was quieter now, the air thick with tension. It was as if the very trees were watching them, waiting for something. Kaelen's hand tightened around the hilt of his sword, his senses alert for any sign of danger.

As they walked, Kaelen couldn't shake the feeling that they were not alone. He had felt it in the temple, and now it was even stronger. The sense that something was watching them, something that didn't belong in this world.

They had been walking for hours when they finally emerged from the forest into a small clearing. The sun was beginning to set, casting long shadows across the ground. Kaelen paused, scanning the clearing for any sign of movement, but there was nothing.

"We should rest here for the night," Alyssa suggested, her voice tinged with exhaustion. "It's too dangerous to keep going in the dark."

Kaelen hesitated, his instincts screaming at him to keep moving. But he knew she was right. They were both exhausted, and they needed to be at their best if they were to face whatever dangers lay ahead.

"Alright," Kaelen agreed, though reluctance tinged his voice. "But we need to be ready to move at a moment's notice."

Alyssa nodded, already setting down her pack. "I'll set up camp. You should rest."

Kaelen wanted to protest, but the exhaustion was catching up with him. The adrenaline that had fueled him in the temple was wearing off, leaving him feeling weak and drained.

"Alright," he agreed, though he knew sleep would be elusive.

As Alyssa set up their makeshift camp, Kaelen sat down on a fallen log, his mind still racing. The gauntlet weighed heavily in his pack, a constant reminder of the power it held. He had felt its potential, its ability to bend time to his will. He also knew the dangers that came with it. The power could consume him, twist him into something he didn't recognize.

He had to try. He had to bring Elias back. It was the only way to make things right.

As the sun dipped below the horizon, plunging the clearing into darkness, Kaelen felt a chill settle over him. The sense of unease that had been growing all day was stronger now, a tangible presence that made the hairs on the back of his neck stand on end.

He glanced at Alyssa, who was sitting by the fire, her expression thoughtful. She had always been the voice of reason, the one who kept him grounded. Even she couldn't deny the power of the gauntlet, the possibilities it presented.

"Alyssa," Kaelen began, his voice quiet. "Do you think... do you think we're doing the right thing?"

Alyssa looked up at him, her eyes filled with the same doubt that had been gnawing at him since they left the temple. "I don't know, Kaelen. I really don't know. I do know that we have to be careful. This power… it's dangerous. It could destroy us if we're not careful."

Kaelen nodded, though the weight of the gauntlet in his pack was a constant reminder of the risks they were taking. "I know. I have to do this, Alyssa. I have to try."

Alyssa reached out, placing a hand on his arm. "I understand, Kaelen. And I'll be with you every step of the way. Please, promise me you won't let this power consume you."

Kaelen met her gaze, seeing the fear and concern in her eyes. "I promise, Alyssa. I won't let it consume me."

Even as he made that promise, he couldn't shake the feeling that something had already changed within him. The power of the gauntlet had awakened something, a force that he couldn't quite control.

As the night deepened, Kaelen lay down on his bedroll, his mind racing with thoughts of what lay ahead. The path they had chosen was fraught with danger, and the power of the gauntlet was both a blessing and a curse. It was his only chance to bring Elias back, to make things right.

Chapter 3

Kaelen woke with a start, his body drenched in sweat despite the cool morning air. His heart pounded in his chest as the remnants of a dream clung to his consciousness—a dream that felt more like a memory, or perhaps a vision. In it, he had seen himself standing in a vast, desolate landscape, the sky dark and filled with swirling clouds. The ground beneath his feet had cracked and splintered, as if the earth itself was being torn apart by some unseen force. In his hand, the gauntlet pulsed with a terrifying energy, and before him, a shadowy figure loomed, its eyes glowing with an unnatural light.

The figure had spoken, its voice a low, rumbling whisper that echoed in Kaelen's mind even now. "You cannot escape your destiny, Kaelen. Time will bend to my will, and you will be the one to bring about its end."

Kaelen shivered, rubbing his hands over his face as he tried to shake off the lingering effects of the dream. It had felt so real, so vivid, as if it was a glimpse of a future that was not yet written but could be. He glanced at the gauntlet, lying beside him on the bedroll. The metal surface was cool and smooth, the intricate patterns etched into it catching the first light of dawn. It seemed innocuous enough now, he could still feel the power within it, the way it had surged through him when he first touched it.

Alyssa stirred beside him, her breathing even and slow as she slept. She looked peaceful; her features relaxed in the dim light. Kaelen envied her calm, her ability to rest without the weight of the world pressing down on her shoulders. He wished he could close his eyes and find that same peace, but his mind was too restless, too burdened by the knowledge of what lay ahead.

He stood quietly, careful not to wake Alyssa, and moved to the edge of their campsite. The forest was still and silent, the trees casting long shadows across the ground. There was a chill in the air, a reminder that the seasons were changing, and soon the warmth of summer would give way to the crispness of autumn. But Kaelen barely noticed the cold; his thoughts were elsewhere, consumed by the vision he had seen.

He could still feel the presence of the shadowy figure, the way it had seemed to reach into his mind and pull at his deepest fears. Who—or what—was it? And why had it spoken of his destiny, of time bending to its will? Kaelen had always believed that he was in control of his own fate, that he could choose his path. Now, for the first time, he felt as if that control was slipping away, as if he was being pulled toward something he could not escape.

The rustling of leaves behind him drew Kaelen out of his thoughts. He turned to see Alyssa sitting up, rubbing sleep from her eyes as she looked around the campsite. She smiled faintly when she saw him, though it quickly faded as she noticed the tension in his posture.

"Kaelen? Is everything alright?" Alyssa's voice was soft, still heavy with sleep.

Kaelen hesitated, unsure whether to share his dream with her. He didn't want to worry her more than she already was, but the memory of the vision was too strong to ignore. Finally, he nodded slowly and walked back to where she sat, lowering himself onto the bedroll beside her.

"I had a dream," he began, his voice quiet. "Or maybe it was more than that. It felt like... like a vision of something that could happen."

Alyssa's brow furrowed in concern as she listened. "What did you see?"

Kaelen took a deep breath, trying to put the vision into words. "I was standing in a place I didn't recognize—somewhere barren and empty, like the earth had been ripped apart. The sky was dark, filled with these swirling clouds, and there was this... figure. A shadowy figure, like it was made of darkness itself. It spoke to me, told me that I couldn't escape my destiny, that time would bend to its will... and that I would be the one to bring about its end."

Alyssa's eyes widened slightly, and she reached out to place a comforting hand on his arm. "Kaelen, which sounds... terrifying. Do you think it's connected to the gauntlet?"

Kaelen nodded slowly, his gaze drifting to the artifact lying beside him. "It has to be. Ever since I touched it, I've felt… different. Like I'm seeing things I shouldn't be seeing, things that haven't happened yet. What if they're not just visions? What if they're warnings?"

Alyssa was silent for a moment, her expression thoughtful. "The gauntlet is powerful, Kaelen. We've both seen what it can do, and we both know that power like that always comes with a cost. Maybe these visions are a way of showing you the consequences of using it."

Kaelen swallowed hard, the weight of her words settling heavily on him. "What if I have no choice? What if using the gauntlet is the only way to bring Elias back?"

Alyssa's grip on his arm tightened slightly. "I understand how much you want to save him, Kaelen. You have to think about what it might cost you. What it might cost all of us. If these visions are warnings, then maybe they're telling you that the price of using the gauntlet is too high."

Kaelen stared at the ground, his thoughts a tangled mess of conflicting emotions. He wanted to believe that he could save Elias without losing himself in the process, but the vision had shaken him to his core. What if Alyssa was right? What if the power of the gauntlet was too dangerous to control?

"I don't know what to do, Alyssa," he admitted, his voice barely above a whisper. "I feel like I'm being pulled in two directions—between the past and the future, between what I want and what I fear."

Alyssa moved closer, wrapping her arms around him in a comforting embrace. "We'll figure it out together, Kaelen. You don't have to face this alone."

Kaelen leaned into her, closing his eyes as he let himself take comfort in her presence. For a moment, the weight of his burden lifted, and he allowed himself to simply be, to forget about the gauntlet and the visions and the shadowy figure that haunted his dreams.

The moment was fleeting, and all too soon, the reality of their situation came crashing back down on him. He pulled away, though he kept one hand entwined with Alyssa's, finding solace in her touch.

"We should get moving," he said quietly. "The longer we stay here, the more vulnerable we are."

Alyssa nodded in agreement, though Kaelen could see the concern still lingering in her eyes. She didn't say anything more as they packed up their campsite, but Kaelen knew that the conversation they had just had would not be the last. The questions that plagued him were not ones that could be easily answered, and he could sense that Alyssa shared his unease.

As they set off once more, the forest around them seemed darker, more foreboding than before. The trees cast long shadows that stretched across the path, their branches intertwining overhead like the bars of a cage. The air was thick with the scent of damp earth and decaying leaves, and the sounds of the forest were muted, as if the very ground they walked on was holding its breath.

Kaelen kept his hand close to the hilt of his sword, his senses on high alert. The unease that had settled over him the night before had not lessened; if anything, it had grown stronger, a constant prickling at the back of his mind. He could feel the gauntlet in his pack, its presence a weight that seemed to drag him down with every step.

Alyssa was quiet as they walked, her eyes scanning the forest around them with a wary intensity. Kaelen knew she was on edge, just as he was, and he couldn't help but wonder if she was feeling the same sense of being watched that he had felt the night before.

The hours passed slowly, the forest growing denser and darker with each step. The path they followed was narrow and winding, the trees pressing in on them from all sides. The air was thick with moisture, the ground beneath their feet soft and treacherous.

As they rounded a bend in the path, Kaelen suddenly froze, his hand shooting out to stop Alyssa in her tracks. She looked at him in confusion, but Kaelen held up a finger to his lips, signaling for her to be silent.

There was something ahead, just beyond the next bend. Kaelen could feel it—a presence that sent a chill down his spine. He strained his ears, listening for any sound, but the forest was deathly silent.

Slowly, Kaelen reached for his sword, the metal hissing softly as it slid from its sheath. Alyssa followed his lead, her hand gripping the hilt of her dagger as she crouched low, ready to spring into action at a moment's notice.

They moved cautiously; their steps silent as they crept toward the bend in the path. Kaelen's heart pounded in his chest, his senses on high alert as he prepared for whatever lay ahead.

As they rounded the corner, Kaelen's breath caught in his throat. The path ahead was blocked by a group of figures, their bodies cloaked in shadow. Their faces were obscured by hoods, but Kaelen could see the glint of metal in their hands—blades that gleamed in the dim light.

For a moment, neither side moved, the tension between them palpable. Then, without warning, the figures lunged forward, their weapons raised as they charged.

Kaelen barely had time to react, his sword flashing up to deflect the first blow. The force of the impact sent a jolt up his arm, but he held his ground, pushing back against his attacker. Alyssa was beside him in an instant, her dagger slashing through the air as she fended off another assailant.

The battle was chaotic, a blur of flashing blades and frenzied movement. Kaelen's heart raced as he fought, his mind focused solely on survival. Even as he parried and struck, a part of him couldn't shake the feeling that something was wrong— something about these attackers was different, unnatural.

It wasn't until one of the figures grabbed his arm, the gauntlet sparking to life in response, that Kaelen understood. These were not ordinary men—they were members of the Legion of Shadows, a group of rogue time travelers who had been corrupted by the power they sought to control.

The realization sent a surge of fear through Kaelen, but it also fueled his resolve. He couldn't let them take the gauntlet, couldn't let them use its power for their own ends. With a roar of determination, he pushed back against his attacker, using the gauntlet to channel a burst of energy that sent the figure flying backward.

The force of the blast was enough to create a ripple in the air, a distortion that warped the space around them. Kaelen could feel the strain it placed on the fabric of time, the way it threatened to unravel everything around them.

He didn't stop. He couldn't afford to hold back, not when the gauntlet was the only thing keeping them alive. With each swing of his sword, he channeled more of the gauntlet's power, using it to enhance his strength, to move faster, to strike harder.

The battle raged on, the forest around them trembling with the force of their fight. Kaelen could feel the gauntlet growing hotter, its energy building to a dangerous level. He knew he was pushing it too far, but he couldn't stop—not when the Legion of Shadows was so close to taking everything from him.

Finally, with one last burst of energy, Kaelen drove the remaining attackers back, sending them crashing into the trees. The force of the blast was enough to knock him off his feet, the gauntlet sparking and crackling as it struggled to contain the power he had unleashed.

When the dust settled, Kaelen was left gasping for breath, his body trembling with exhaustion. The members of the Legion of Shadows lay scattered around him, their forms still and unmoving.

Alyssa was at his side in an instant, her hands gripping his shoulders as she helped him sit up. "Kaelen, are you alright?"

He nodded weakly, though his body still shook from the strain of using the gauntlet. "I... I'm fine. Just... give me a moment."

Alyssa's eyes were filled with worry as she examined him, but she said nothing, her grip on his shoulders firm. Kaelen could feel the lingering traces of the gauntlet's power coursing through his veins, like a distant echo that refused to fade.

"We need to get out of here," Alyssa said urgently, her voice tinged with fear. "Before more of them show up."

Kaelen nodded, his mind still reeling from the battle. He knew she was right—they couldn't stay here. The Legion of Shadows was still out there, and they would stop at nothing to get the gauntlet.

As they staggered to their feet, Kaelen couldn't help but glance back at the fallen members of the Legion. There was something unsettling about the way they lay so still, their bodies unnaturally contorted as if the blast had twisted them into something inhuman.

Alyssa tugged at his arm, pulling him away from the clearing. "Come on, Kaelen. We need to go."

He nodded, forcing himself to turn away from the carnage. They moved quickly; their steps unsteady as they fled the scene of the battle. Kaelen could feel the weight of the gauntlet in his pack, a constant reminder of the power he had just unleashed.

As they made their way through the forest, Kaelen couldn't shake the feeling that something had changed. The battle had awakened something within him, something that he wasn't sure he could control.

They walked for what felt like hours, the forest around them growing darker and more oppressive with each step. Kaelen's mind was a blur of thoughts and emotions, the events of the past few hours replaying in his head over and over again.

Finally, they emerged from the forest into a small clearing. The sun had set, plunging the world into darkness, but the moon had risen, casting a pale light over the landscape.

Kaelen and Alyssa collapsed onto the ground, their bodies trembling with exhaustion. The air was cool and crisp, a stark contrast to the heat of the battle they had just fought.

For a long time, neither of them spoke, the silence between them heavy with unspoken fears. Kaelen could feel the weight of the gauntlet in his pack, a constant reminder of the power he had just unleashed.

Finally, Alyssa broke the silence, her voice quiet but firm. "Kaelen, we need to talk about what happened back there."

Kaelen nodded, though he wasn't sure he was ready to face the reality of what he had just done. "I know. I pushed the gauntlet too far."

Alyssa's gaze was intense as she looked at him, her eyes filled with concern. "Kaelen, you almost lost control. That power... it's dangerous. You can't keep using it like that."

Kaelen sighed, running a hand through his hair as he tried to gather his thoughts. "I know, Alyssa. But what choice do I have? The Legion of Shadows isn't going to stop. They'll keep coming after us until they get the gauntlet."

Alyssa reached out, placing a hand on his arm. "I understand that, Kaelen. But you have to be careful. That power... it could destroy you."

Kaelen met her gaze, seeing the fear and concern in her eyes. "I'll be careful, Alyssa. I promise."

Even as he made that promise, Kaelen couldn't shake the feeling that something had already changed within him. The power of the gauntlet had awakened something, a force that he couldn't quite control.

As they sat in the clearing, the moon casting long shadows across the ground, Kaelen felt the weight of the gauntlet pressing down on him, a constant reminder of the price of the power he now possessed.

The road ahead was fraught with danger, and Kaelen knew that the battle they had just fought was only the beginning. The Legion of Shadows was still out there, and they would stop at nothing to take the gauntlet.

Kaelen was determined. He would not let the gauntlet fall into the wrong hands. He would not let the power consume him.

And most of all, he would not let the shadowy figure from his vision control his destiny.

As the night deepened and the stars flickered overhead, Kaelen and Alyssa prepared to continue their journey. The path ahead was uncertain, but one thing was clear: the price of power was high, and Kaelen was willing to pay it—whatever the cost.

Chapter 4

The forest was eerily silent as Kaelen and Alyssa pressed on, the weight of their recent battle with the Legion of Shadows hanging heavy in the air. Every step felt labored, as if the earth itself was resisting their progress. The wounds from the fight stung, and though they had escaped with their lives, the victory felt hollow. The Legion had been relentless, their attacks coordinated, almost as if they had known Kaelen and Alyssa's every move. And then there was the gauntlet—the power it had unleashed had saved them, but at what cost?

Kaelen's hand trembled slightly as he adjusted the strap of his pack, feeling the gauntlet's cold weight against his back.

The memory of the power coursing through him, wild and untamed, sent a shiver down his spine. It had felt… intoxicating, as if he had touched the very fabric of time itself. With that power had come a darkness, a voice whispering in the depths of his mind, urging him to take control, to bend time to his will.

He glanced at Alyssa, who walked beside him, her eyes scanning the forest with a mix of determination and wariness. She had always been strong, grounded, her focus unyielding even in the face of danger. Now, there was a tension in her posture, a shadow of fear that hadn't been there before. Kaelen knew she was worried about him—about the gauntlet, and what it was doing to him.

"Alyssa," Kaelen began, his voice rough from the silence they had maintained since the battle. "Do you think… do you think we're doing the right thing?"

Alyssa slowed her pace, turning to look at him fully. Her eyes softened, the worry in them clear. "Kaelen, you know why we're doing this. You know what's at stake."

"I know," Kaelen said, his voice barely above a whisper. "I can't shake the feeling that… that I'm losing myself. The power of the gauntlet—it's overwhelming. I don't know how much longer I can control it."

Alyssa reached out, placing a comforting hand on his arm. "We'll figure this out together, Kaelen. You're not alone in this. We have to keep moving. The Legion won't stop coming after us, and we need to stay ahead of them."

Kaelen nodded, though the doubt gnawed at him. He knew Alyssa was right—they couldn't afford to stop, not now. The weight of the gauntlet was a constant reminder of the power he wielded, and the danger it posed.

As they continued through the dense forest, Kaelen couldn't shake the feeling that something was wrong. The air was thick with an unnatural stillness, the usual sounds of the forest—birds calling, leaves rustling—absent. It was as if the entire world was holding its breath, waiting for something to happen.

Then, without warning, the ground beneath them shifted, the earth trembling as if in response to some unseen force. Kaelen stumbled, grabbing a nearby tree for support as the world around him seemed to blur and distort.

"What's happening?" Alyssa gasped, her eyes wide with alarm.

Kaelen struggled to regain his balance, his heart racing as the forest around them warped and twisted, the trees bending in unnatural ways. The air grew thick, heavy with the scent of ozone, and the light around them flickered, as if the very fabric of reality was tearing at the seams.

"It's the gauntlet," Kaelen realized, his voice tinged with fear. "The power... it's causing these anomalies."

Alyssa's grip tightened on his arm. "We have to get out of here, Kaelen. Before it gets worse."

Even as she spoke, the anomalies grew stronger. The trees around them began to pulse with an eerie light, their shapes shifting and blurring as if they were being pulled in and out of time. The ground beneath them buckled, cracking open to reveal glimpses of other places, other times—images that flickered in and out of existence like fragments of a shattered mirror.

Kaelen's mind reeled as he tried to make sense of what he was seeing. There were moments of his past, memories he had long buried, playing out before him—his childhood with Elias, their first expedition together, the day they had found the ancient tomb that had led to Elias's death. There were also visions of futures that had never come to pass, alternate realities where things had gone differently. In one, he saw himself standing over Elias's grave, the gauntlet clutched in his hand, a look of despair etched on his face. In another, he saw Alyssa lying lifeless on the ground, the Legion of Shadows standing over her, their faces hidden in shadow.

"No!" Kaelen cried out, shaking his head as if to dispel the visions. They continued to assault his senses, each one more vivid and terrifying than the last.

"Kaelen, listen to me!" Alyssa's voice cut through the chaos, grounding him. "You have to focus. We need to get out of here—now!"

Kaelen nodded, forcing himself to push the visions aside. He grabbed Alyssa's hand, pulling her forward as they began to run, their footsteps echoing through the warped forest. The ground continued to tremble beneath them, the anomalies growing more intense with each passing moment. Kaelen could feel the gauntlet pulsing against his back, its power straining to break free.

They ran blindly through the forest, the world around them a blur of distorted images and flickering light. Kaelen's heart pounded in his chest, his breath coming in ragged gasps as they pushed forward, desperate to escape the temporal chaos that threatened to consume them.

No matter how fast they ran, the anomalies followed, warping the landscape around them. Trees twisted into impossible shapes, their branches reaching out like skeletal hands. The ground beneath them cracked open, revealing glimpses of other times and places, each more nightmarish than the last.

Kaelen's mind raced as he tried to think of a way to stop the anomalies, to control the power of the gauntlet before it tore the world apart. The more he tried to focus, the more the voices in his head grew louder, drowning out his thoughts. They were whispers at first, faint echoes of the past and future, but they quickly grew into a cacophony of sound, each voice vying for his attention.

"Kaelen... Kaelen... You cannot escape your destiny... Time will bend to my will..."

The voice from his vision—the shadowy figure that had haunted his dreams—echoed in his mind, its words twisting and distorting like the world around him. Kaelen clutched his head, trying to block out the voice, but it only grew louder, more insistent.

"Kaelen, stop!" Alyssa's voice broke through the noise, pulling him back to the present. She was standing a few steps ahead, her eyes wide with fear as she reached out to him. "You have to fight it! Don't let the gauntlet take control!"

Kaelen nodded weakly, forcing himself to focus on her voice. He took a deep breath, trying to calm his racing heart as he reached for the gauntlet. The moment his fingers touched the metal, a jolt of energy shot through him, and the voices in his head fell silent.

The forest around them began to stabilize, the anomalies slowly fading as Kaelen regained control of the gauntlet's power. The ground beneath them solidified, the trees returning to their natural shapes as the flickering light dimmed.

Kaelen fell to his knees, gasping for breath as the last of the anomalies vanished. The gauntlet was still warm to the touch, but the wild, uncontrollable energy that had surged through it was gone.

Alyssa was at his side in an instant, her hands gripping his shoulders as she helped him sit up. "Kaelen, are you alright?"

He nodded weakly, though his body still trembled from the strain of controlling the gauntlet. "I... I think so. But that was... it was too close."

Alyssa's eyes were filled with concern as she looked at him. "Kaelen, you can't keep doing this. The gauntlet's power is too much for you to handle. We need to find another way."

Kaelen shook his head, his expression pained. "I don't know if there is another way, Alyssa. The gauntlet... it's the only thing that can help us. But I don't know how much longer I can control it."

Alyssa's grip tightened on his shoulders. "We'll figure it out, Kaelen. But we can't let the gauntlet destroy you. We need to find a way to control it before it's too late."

Kaelen nodded, though the doubt still gnawed at him. He knew Alyssa was right—they needed to find a way to control the gauntlet's power before it consumed him. The voice in his head, the shadowy figure that had spoken of his destiny, haunted him. Was this truly his fate? To wield a power that could destroy the world.

As they sat in the clearing, the forest around them eerily quiet, Kaelen couldn't shake the feeling that something was watching them. He glanced around, his hand instinctively reaching for his sword, but the forest was empty, the shadows still.

Then, out of the corner of his eye, Kaelen saw movement—a figure, barely visible in the fading light, standing at the edge of the clearing. His heart skipped a beat as he turned to face the figure, his hand tightening on the hilt of his sword.

"Alyssa," he whispered, his voice tense. "We're not alone."

Alyssa followed his gaze, her eyes narrowing as she spotted the figure. "Who's there?"

The figure stepped forward, emerging from the shadows. It was a man, tall and lean, his face partially hidden by a hood. His clothes were tattered, his boots worn from years of travel, but there was something about him—something familiar.

Kaelen's grip on his sword tightened as the man approached, his eyes locked on the gauntlet strapped to Kaelen's back.

"You've come far, Kaelen Mercer," the man said, his voice low and gravelly. "But you're playing with forces you don't understand."

Kaelen's heart raced as he studied the man, trying to place where he had seen him before. There was something about the man's presence, something that set off alarms in his mind.

"Who are you?" Kaelen demanded, his voice steady despite the tension that gripped him. "What do you want?"

The man chuckled, though there was no humor in it. "I've been following your progress for some time now. I know what you seek, and I know the power you carry. The gauntlet is a dangerous tool, Kaelen, one that can easily destroy you if you're not careful."

Alyssa stepped forward, her eyes narrowing. "And how do you know that? Who are you?"

The man's gaze shifted to Alyssa, his expression unreadable. "I am someone who once sought the same power you now hold. I was a Time Keeper, like you, Kaelen. But I learned the hard way that some forces are better left untouched."

Kaelen's breath caught in his throat. A former Time Keeper? This man had once been part of the same order that Kaelen had sought to join before Elias's death. Why had he left? What had driven him away?

"What happened to you?" Kaelen asked, his voice tinged with curiosity. "Why did you leave the Time Keepers?"

The man's expression darkened, his gaze drifting to the ground. "I made a mistake—one that nearly destroyed everything. I thought I could control the power of the gauntlet, bend time to my will. I was wrong. The gauntlet... it changes you. It consumes you. And once it has its hold on you, there's no going back."

Alyssa's eyes widened with alarm as she glanced at Kaelen. "Kaelen, we have to be careful. This man... he's warning us."

Kaelen swallowed hard, the man's words resonating with the fears that had plagued him since he first touched the gauntlet. "If you know so much, then tell me—how do I control it? How do I stop it from consuming me?"

The man's gaze shifted back to Kaelen, his expression serious. "There is no easy answer, Kaelen. The gauntlet's power is tied to your very essence, to your will and your strength. It also feeds on your fears, your doubts. If you let those consume you, the gauntlet will follow suit."

Kaelen felt a chill run down his spine. The man's words echoed the thoughts that had haunted him since the vision—the fear that he was losing control, that the gauntlet's power was too much for him to manage.

"Then what do I do?" Kaelen asked, his voice trembling with desperation. "How do I stop it?"

The man's expression softened slightly, though his eyes remained wary. "You must learn to master your fears, Kaelen. The gauntlet's power is a double-edged sword—it can be a great tool, but it can also be a great burden. You must find the balance, or it will destroy you."

Kaelen nodded, though his mind was still reeling from the man's revelations. He knew the gauntlet was powerful, but he hadn't realized just how dangerous it truly was. The man's words confirmed his worst fears—that the gauntlet was not just a tool, but a force that could consume him if he wasn't careful.

As the man turned to leave, Kaelen felt a surge of urgency. "Wait—what about the Shadow Keeper? Do you know anything about him?"

The man paused, his expression darkening once more. "The Shadow Keeper is not someone you want to cross paths with, Kaelen. He is a force of destruction, a being who has embraced the darkness within him. If you're not careful, you'll find yourself following in his footsteps."

Kaelen's heart pounded in his chest as the man's words sank in. The Shadow Keeper—a name that had haunted the whispers of the Time Keepers for years. But what was his connection to him? What did he want with the gauntlet?

Before Kaelen could ask any more questions, the man turned and disappeared into the shadows, leaving Kaelen and Alyssa alone in the clearing.

For a long moment, they stood in silence, the weight of the man's words hanging heavy between them.

"Alyssa," Kaelen began, his voice trembling. "What if he's right? What if the gauntlet... what if it destroys me?"

Alyssa moved closer; her eyes filled with determination. "Then we'll find a way to stop it, Kaelen. We'll figure this out together. You're not alone in this."

Kaelen nodded, though the doubt still gnawed at him. The gauntlet's power was a dangerous force, one that could easily consume him if he wasn't careful. With Alyssa by his side, he felt a glimmer of hope—a hope that maybe, just maybe, they could find a way to control it.

As they prepared to leave the clearing, Kaelen couldn't shake the feeling that they were being watched. The forest around them was silent, the shadows deep and impenetrable. The memory of the man's words lingered in his mind, a reminder of the dangers that lay ahead.

The Shadow Keeper was out there, somewhere, watching and waiting. And if Kaelen wasn't careful, he would fall into the same darkness that had consumed so many before him.

As they stepped back onto the path, Kaelen felt a renewed sense of purpose. He would not let the gauntlet control him. He would find a way to master its power, to use it for good.

And he would do whatever it took to protect Alyssa, to keep her safe from the forces that sought to destroy them.

The road ahead was long and treacherous, but Kaelen was determined. He would not let the gauntlet destroy him. He would not let the Shadow Keeper win.

As the night deepened and the stars flickered overhead, Kaelen and Alyssa continued their journey, the weight of the gauntlet pressing down on them like a dark shadow. Even in the face of overwhelming odds, Kaelen felt a spark of hope.

They would find a way. They had to.

For Elias, for the future, for each other—they would find a way.

Chapter 5

The air around Kaelen and Alyssa seemed to pulse with a life of its own as they ventured deeper into the forest, a place where time no longer followed the rules they once knew. The trees around them twisted in unnatural shapes, their branches swaying as if moved by an invisible hand. The ground beneath their feet was soft and unstable, shifting subtly with every step, making it difficult to maintain balance.

Kaelen's breath came in shallow bursts, his senses heightened by the ever-present feeling that something was terribly wrong. The gauntlet weighed heavily on his back, its power humming in rhythm with the strange energies that warped the landscape around them. He had felt its pull since the moment he had first touched it, but now, that pull was stronger than ever, as if the gauntlet was urging him forward, deeper into the heart of the distortion.

Alyssa walked beside him, her eyes constantly scanning their surroundings. She had grown increasingly quiet since their encounter with the mysterious figure who had warned them about the gauntlet and the Shadow Keeper. Kaelen could sense her fear, her worry that the power he now wielded was changing him in ways neither of them fully understood.

The path ahead was barely visible, obscured by the thick undergrowth and the strange, shimmering light that filtered through the trees. It was as if the forest was alive, breathing in sync with the pulsing energy that emanated from the gauntlet.

Kaelen reached out to steady himself against a nearby tree, but the moment his hand touched the rough bark, it crumbled to dust, disintegrating into nothingness. He pulled his hand back in shock, watching as the tree reformed itself, growing rapidly from the ground up, its branches stretching out in unnatural angles.

"This place… it's wrong," Alyssa whispered, her voice trembling. "It's like time is… collapsing in on itself."

Kaelen nodded; his mouth dry as he tried to find his voice. "It's the gauntlet. I can feel it… it's connected to all of this."

Alyssa turned to him; her expression filled with concern. "Kaelen, we have to be careful. We don't know what the gauntlet is capable of—what it's doing to you."

Kaelen met her gaze, the weight of her words pressing down on him. He knew she was right. The gauntlet's power was growing stronger, more insistent, and with it, the visions that plagued his mind had become more vivid, more real. They were no longer just fleeting images; they were tangible, almost like memories of a life he had never lived.

They continued onward, the landscape around them growing more twisted and chaotic with each step. The trees no longer followed any natural order, their trunks spiraling upwards into the sky before curving back down to the ground. The sky itself was a patchwork of colors—vibrant blues, deep purples, and fiery reds—blending together in a way that made Kaelen's head spin.

As they walked, Kaelen's vision began to blur, the edges of reality warping as the gauntlet's power pulsed against his back. He could feel it, deep in his bones, the pull of time bending and shifting around him. The visions began to creep in again, stronger this time, seizing control of his senses.

In one moment, he was standing in a vast desert, the sun beating down on him with relentless heat. The sand beneath his feet was scorching, the air dry and suffocating. He looked around, disoriented, before realizing he was not alone. Elias stood before him, alive and well, his face etched with concern.

"Kaelen, you can't keep doing this," Elias said, his voice strained. "You have to let go of the past."

Kaelen blinked, the words not making sense. "But… Elias, I'm doing this for you. I have to save you."

Elias shook his head, his expression sad. "You're losing yourself, Kaelen. The gauntlet is changing you—twisting your mind. You have to stop before it's too late."

The vision shifted, the desert melting away to reveal a dark, stormy landscape. Kaelen stood on the edge of a cliff, the wind howling around him. Below, the ocean churned violently, waves crashing against the jagged rocks. He could see himself standing at the edge, the gauntlet glowing with an ominous light.

Alyssa was there, too, reaching out to him, her voice filled with desperation. "Kaelen, please! Don't do this! You're going to destroy everything!"

Kaelen shook his head, trying to shake off the vision, but the pull of the gauntlet was too strong. The visions continued to flood his mind, each one more vivid, more intense than the last. He saw himself in countless different scenarios—some where he succeeded in saving Elias, others where he failed spectacularly, the world crumbling around him.

The weight of the visions was overwhelming, and Kaelen could feel his grip on reality slipping. He stumbled forward, barely aware of Alyssa's voice calling out to him. The world around him was a blur of colors and sounds, the gauntlet's power resonating in his ears like a deafening hum.

Then, suddenly, everything went silent.

Kaelen found himself standing in a peaceful meadow, the sun shining brightly overhead. The air was warm and fragrant, filled with the scent of blooming flowers. Birds sang in the trees, their melodies a soothing balm to his frayed nerves.

He looked around, disoriented, before realizing that Elias was there, too, sitting on a blanket under a large oak tree. He was smiling, his face relaxed and content, as if nothing in the world could trouble him.

"Elias?" Kaelen whispered, his heart pounding in his chest. "Is this… real?"

Elias looked up at him, his smile widening. "It could be, Kaelen. This is what you've been fighting for, isn't it? A chance to save me, to bring back the life we had."

Kaelen felt tears sting his eyes as he moved toward his brother, the weight of the gauntlet forgotten. "I've missed you so much, Elias. I would do anything to have your back."

Elias's smile faltered, his expression turning serious. "But at what cost, Kaelen? The gauntlet's power is dangerous. It's not meant to be wielded by just anyone."

Kaelen hesitated, the warmth of the meadow suddenly feeling oppressive. "But I can control it, Elias. I can make this real."

Elias stood, his expression filled with a mixture of sadness and determination. "You're stronger than this, Kaelen. You don't need the gauntlet to find peace. You need to let go."

Kaelen shook his head, the temptation of the vision pulling at him. "I can't just let go, Elias. I have to save you."

Elias stepped closer, his hand resting on Kaelen's shoulder. "I'm already gone, Kaelen. You can't change the past, no matter how hard you try. But you can choose to live in the present—to protect the people who are still with you."

Kaelen's breath hitched, the reality of Elias's words cutting through the fog of the vision. He could feel the gauntlet's power pulling at him, tempting him to give in, to make the vision real. Elias's presence, his words, were like a lifeline, grounding Kaelen in the present.

"I... I don't know if I can do it," Kaelen whispered, his voice breaking. "I don't know if I can let go."

Elias's smile returned, softer this time, filled with understanding. "You're stronger than you think, Kaelen. But you have to choose—me, or the future you want to protect."

Kaelen felt a tear slip down his cheek as he looked at his brother, the vision beginning to fade. "I'm sorry, Elias."

The meadow dissolved into mist, and Kaelen found himself back in the forest, the gauntlet's weight heavy on his back. The colors of the landscape were muted, the air thick with tension. Alyssa was standing in front of him, her hands gripping his arms tightly, her face etched with worry.

"Kaelen! Are you with me?" Alyssa's voice was filled with urgency, pulling him fully back to reality.

Kaelen blinked, the last remnants of the vision dissipating as he focused on Alyssa's face. "I… I'm here."

Alyssa's grip tightened, her eyes searching his for any sign of the Kaelen she knew. "You have to fight it, Kaelen. The gauntlet is trying to control you, to twist your mind. You can't let it win."

Kaelen nodded weakly, his body trembling with the effort of resisting the gauntlet's pull. "It's so strong, Alyssa. I don't know how much longer I can hold on."

Alyssa's expression softened, her concern evident. "You're not alone, Kaelen. We'll get through this together. You have to trust me—trust yourself."

Kaelen took a deep breath, the tension in his chest easing slightly as he focused on Alyssa's words. "I trust you, Alyssa. I just… I don't want to lose you."

Alyssa's eyes glistened with unshed tears as she cupped his face in her hands. "You won't lose me, Kaelen. I'm right here."

Kaelen closed his eyes, the warmth of Alyssa's touch grounding him in the present. For a moment, the pull of the gauntlet faded, replaced by a sense of calm. He could feel the power within him, still strong, still dangerous, but it was tempered by the bond he shared with Alyssa.

They stood there for a long moment, the forest around them silent and still. The distorted landscape had begun to stabilize, the unnatural colors and shifting ground returning to something resembling normalcy. The air was still thick with tension, but it was no longer suffocating, no longer threatening to tear them apart.

Finally, Kaelen pulled away, his gaze steady as he met Alyssa's eyes. "We need to keep moving. The Shadow Keeper's influence is growing stronger—we're running out of time."

Alyssa nodded, though Kaelen could see the worry still etched in her features. "We'll find a way, Kaelen. But you have to promise me that you'll be careful. The gauntlet... it's dangerous. We can't let it consume you."

Kaelen's grip tightened on the strap of his pack, the weight of the gauntlet pressing against him like a constant reminder of the power he wielded. "I promise, Alyssa. I'll fight it."

With renewed determination, they continued onward, the forest around them growing darker as they ventured deeper into the Shadow Keeper's domain. The air grew colder, the trees more twisted and gnarled, their branches clawing at the sky like skeletal hands. The ground beneath their feet was littered with the remnants of a once-thriving forest, now reduced to a barren wasteland.

As they walked, the sense of foreboding grew stronger, the silence around them heavy with the weight of unseen eyes. Kaelen could feel the gauntlet's power resonating in his bones, its pull growing stronger with each step. But he fought against it, focusing on the path ahead, on the mission that had brought them here.

They emerged from the forest into a clearing, the ground beneath their feet cracked and dry. In the center of the clearing stood a village—or what was left of it. The buildings were crumbling, their walls blackened by fire, the roofs caved in. The air was thick with the stench of decay, and the ground was littered with debris—broken furniture, shattered glass, and the charred remains of what had once been people.

Alyssa gasped, her hand flying to her mouth as she took in the devastation. "What… what happened here?"

Kaelen's heart pounded in his chest as he stepped forward, the gauntlet's power pulsing in response to the scene before them. "It's the Shadow Keeper. This is his doing."

Alyssa's eyes were wide with horror as she looked around the village, her voice trembling. "How could anyone do something like this?"

Kaelen clenched his fists, the anger boiling within him. "The Shadow Keeper isn't just anyone. He's a force of destruction, a being who has embraced the darkness within him. This... this is just a glimpse of what he's capable of."

They moved cautiously through the village, their steps careful as they navigated the wreckage. The silence was oppressive, the air thick with the weight of death and despair. Kaelen could feel the gauntlet's power reacting to the scene around them, its energy resonating with the darkness that had consumed the village.

As they reached the center of the village, Kaelen's gaze was drawn to a figure standing in the shadows, partially obscured by the crumbling remains of a building. The figure was tall and slender, its features hidden beneath a dark hood. Kaelen's heart skipped a beat as he realized that the figure was watching them, its gaze piercing through the darkness.

"Alyssa," Kaelen whispered, his voice tense. "We're not alone."

Alyssa followed his gaze, her eyes narrowing as she spotted the figure. "Who... who is that?"

The figure stepped forward, its movements slow and deliberate. As it emerged from the shadows, Kaelen's breath caught in his throat. The figure was not human—its skin was pale and translucent, its eyes glowing with an unnatural light. The air around it seemed to shimmer, as if reality itself was bending to its will.

Kaelen's grip tightened on his sword as he stepped in front of Alyssa, his body tense. "Stay back, Alyssa. This isn't just any ordinary enemy."

The figure's voice was a low, guttural hiss, its words echoing through the clearing. "You are trespassing in the Shadow Keeper's domain. Leave now or face the consequences."

Kaelen's heart pounded in his chest as he met the figure's gaze. "We're not leaving. We're here to stop the Shadow Keeper."

The figure chuckled, a sound that sent chills down Kaelen's spine. "You are foolish to think you can stand against the Shadow Keeper. His power is beyond your comprehension."

Alyssa stepped forward; her voice filled with determination. "We won't let him destroy everything. We'll find a way to stop him."

The figure's glowing eyes narrowed; its voice filled with disdain. "You are nothing but insects, crawling in the shadow of a god. You will be crushed beneath his power."

Kaelen's grip on his sword tightened as he prepared for a fight. The gauntlet's power surged within him, resonating with the darkness that emanated from the figure. He could feel the pull, the temptation to unleash the full force of the gauntlet's power, to obliterate the enemy before them.

He knew the risks. He knew that giving in to the gauntlet's power could have catastrophic consequences. He couldn't afford to lose control—not now, not when so much was at stake.

The figure raised its hand, the air around it is crackling with dark energy. Kaelen braced himself, ready to defend against the attack. Before the figure could strike, a blinding light filled the clearing, forcing Kaelen and Alyssa to shield their eyes.

When the light faded, the figure was gone, leaving only the lingering sense of dread in its wake.

Kaelen lowered his hand, his heart racing as he scanned the clearing. "What… what just happened?"

Alyssa shook her head, her expression filled with confusion. "I don't know. But whatever that was... it's gone now."

Kaelen took a deep breath, the tension in his body easing slightly. The encounter had left him shaken, the reality of the Shadow Keeper's power all too clear. They were dealing with forces beyond their comprehension, forces that could easily destroy them if they weren't careful.

"We need to keep moving," Kaelen said, his voice firm. "The Shadow Keeper's influence is growing stronger. We don't have much time."

Alyssa nodded, though Kaelen could see the fear in her eyes. "We'll find a way, Kaelen. We have to."

As they left the village behind, Kaelen couldn't shake the feeling that they were being watched, that the Shadow Keeper's gaze was fixed on them, waiting for the moment to strike. The road ahead was treacherous, and the stakes had never been higher. Kaelen was determined. He would not let the gauntlet consume him. He would not let the Shadow Keeper win.

The journey was far from over, but Kaelen knew that they had to keep going—keep fighting—if they were to have any hope of saving the future. The gauntlet's power was a double-edged sword, a tool that could either save them or destroy them. It was up to Kaelen to decide which path he would take.

As the darkness closed in around them, Kaelen steeled himself for the battle ahead. The Shadow Keeper's grasp was tightening, but Kaelen was determined to break free.

And he would do whatever it took to protect Alyssa, to protect the future, to protect the world from the darkness that threatened to consume it.

Chapter 6

Kaelen and Alyssa moved cautiously through the dense forest, the shadows of the trees stretching long across the ground as the sun dipped lower in the sky. The air was thick with anticipation, each rustle of leaves and snap of a twig sending a jolt of tension through them. They had been following the clues for hours, piecing together fragments of ancient lore and half-forgotten myths, each step bringing them closer to their goal: the hidden sanctuary of the Time Keepers.

The clues had led them to this remote part of the forest, far from any known paths. The trees here were ancient, their trunks thick and gnarled, their roots twisting through the earth like the veins of some colossal creature. The air was cool and still, carrying with it the scent of damp earth and decaying leaves. It was as if the forest itself was holding its breath, waiting for them to uncover the secrets it had guarded for so long.

Kaelen tightened his grip on the strap of his pack, the weight of the gauntlet a constant reminder of the power he carried. He could feel it pulsing against his back, a steady, rhythmic beat that seemed to resonate with the very air around them. The gauntlet had been growing stronger the closer they came to the sanctuary, its presence a living force that both guided and haunted him.

Beside him, Alyssa was deep in thought, her brow furrowed as she studied the map they had pieced together from ancient texts and the cryptic words of the mysterious figure they had encountered. The map was incomplete, more of a rough sketch than a detailed guide, but it was all they had. And so far, it had led them true.

"According to the map, we should be close," Alyssa murmured, her eyes scanning the forest ahead. "The entrance to the sanctuary is hidden, but it's supposed to be marked by a symbol—something ancient, from the time before the Time Keepers."

Kaelen nodded, though his mind was elsewhere, focused on the weight of the gauntlet and the growing sense of urgency that gnawed at him. The Shadow Keeper's influence was spreading, and they were running out of time. The sooner they found the sanctuary, the sooner they could seek the Time Keepers' help—and perhaps find a way to stop the Shadow Keeper before it was too late.

As they pressed on, the forest around them grew denser, the trees closing in on all sides. The light filtering through the canopy above was dim and muted, casting everything in shades of green and brown. The air was thick with the scent of moss and damp earth, and the ground beneath their feet was soft, giving slightly with each step.

Then, suddenly, Alyssa stopped, her eyes fixed on something ahead. "Kaelen, look."

Kaelen followed her gaze, his breath catching in his throat. Ahead of them, partially hidden by a tangle of roots and vines, was a massive stone archway. The arch was ancient, its surface weathered and worn, but the symbols carved into it were still visible symbols that matched those on the map.

"This is it," Alyssa whispered, her voice filled with awe. "The entrance to the sanctuary."

Kaelen stepped forward, his heart pounding in his chest as he approached the archway. The closer he got, the stronger the pull of the gauntlet became, until it felt as if his entire being was resonating with the power that emanated from the stones.

He reached out, his fingers brushing against the cold surface of the arch. The moment he made contact, a surge of energy shot through him, the symbols on the arch glowing with a faint, ethereal light. The ground beneath them trembled, and the air around them seemed to hum with an otherworldly power.

Alyssa took a step back, her eyes wide with a mixture of fear and wonder. "Kaelen, what's happening?"

Kaelen shook his head, his mind racing as he tried to process the sensation. "I don't know… but I think the gauntlet is reacting to the sanctuary."

As if in response to his words, the archway began to change. The vines that had obscured it slithered away as if pulled by an unseen force, revealing more of the ancient carvings. The ground beneath the arch shifted, the earth moving as a pathway began to reveal itself, leading down into the darkness.

"This is it," Kaelen said, his voice filled with a mix of excitement and trepidation. "The entrance to the Time Keepers' sanctuary."

Alyssa nodded, her expression serious. "Are you ready?"

Kaelen took a deep breath, the weight of the gauntlet pressing down on him like a physical force. "I don't think we have a choice. We need to do this—before it's too late."

Together, they stepped through the archway and onto the path that led into the darkness below. The air grew colder as they descended, the light from the surface fading until they were enveloped in shadow. The path was narrow and steep, the walls of the tunnel close on either side, and the only sound was the soft echo of their footsteps against the stone.

As they moved deeper into the earth, Kaelen could feel the gauntlet's power growing stronger, the connection between it and the sanctuary becoming more pronounced. It was as if the gauntlet was feeding off the energy of the place, growing more potent with each step they took.

The tunnel eventually opened up into a vast chamber, the ceiling so high it was lost in the darkness above. The walls of the chamber were lined with massive stone pillars, each one etched with symbols and runes that glowed faintly in the dim light. At the far end of the chamber, a set of massive doors stood closed, their surface carved with intricate designs that seemed to shift and change as Kaelen and Alyssa approached.

"This must be the entrance to the sanctuary itself," Alyssa said, her voice hushed in the stillness of the chamber. "But how do we open it?"

Kaelen stepped closer to the doors; his gaze drawn to the symbols that adorned them. The gauntlet pulsed against his back, the energy within it resonating with the symbols on the doors. He reached out, his fingers brushing against the cold stone.

The moment he made contact, the gauntlet flared to life, its power surging through him. The symbols on the doors glowed brighter, the air around them humming with energy. Slowly, the doors began to move, grinding open with a deep, rumbling sound that echoed through the chamber.

Kaelen and Alyssa exchanged a glance, their expressions filled with a mixture of excitement and apprehension. This was it—the entrance to the Time Keepers' sanctuary, the place where they would find the answers they sought.

As the doors opened wider, revealing the darkness beyond, Kaelen couldn't shake the feeling that they were stepping into something far greater—and far more dangerous—than they had ever imagined.

They stepped through the doors, the air around them thick with the weight of ancient power. The chamber beyond was vast, stretching out into the darkness, its walls lined with more pillars and symbols that glowed faintly in the dim light. The floor was smooth and polished, reflecting the light of the symbols, and the air was cool and still, as if the entire place was holding its breath.

As they moved deeper into the chamber, Kaelen felt the gauntlet's power intensify, the connection between it and the sanctuary growing stronger. It was as if the very stones of the place were alive, resonating with the same energy that flowed through the gauntlet.

Then, without warning, the air around them began to shift. The symbols on the walls flared to life, glowing brighter until the entire chamber was bathed in an ethereal light. The ground beneath their feet trembled, and the air hummed with a deep, resonant sound that seemed to come from all around them.

Kaelen and Alyssa stopped, their eyes wide as they looked around, trying to understand what was happening. The light grew brighter, the humming louder, until it felt as if the very air was vibrating with energy.

Then, from the center of the chamber, a figure began to materialize, slowly taking shape as the light coalesced around it. The figure was tall and imposing, its features shrouded in shadow, but there was no mistaking the power that emanated from it.

Kaelen's heart pounded in his chest as he realized what—or who—they were facing.

The figure stepped forward, its form solidifying as it emerged from the light. It was an ancient being, its face lined with age, its eyes glowing with an inner light that seemed to pierce through Kaelen's very soul. The being was dressed in robes that shimmered with the same ethereal light that filled the chamber, and its presence filled the air with a sense of immense power and authority.

"Welcome, Kaelen Mercer," the being said, its voice deep and resonant, echoing through the chamber. "You have come far to find this place."

Kaelen swallowed hard; his mouth dry as he struggled to find his voice. "You… you know who I am?"

The being nodded, its gaze fixed on Kaelen. "We have been watching you for some time, Kaelen. The gauntlet you carry is a powerful artifact, one that has been lost to time for many centuries. It is no small feat that you have found it—and brought it here."

Kaelen's mind raced as he tried to process the being's words. "Who are you? Are you one of the Time Keepers?"

The being inclined its head slightly. "I am a guardian of this sanctuary, one of many who protect the knowledge and power that resides within these walls. The Time Keepers themselves are… elsewhere, beyond the reach of this world. Their influence remains, as does their purpose."

Alyssa stepped forward; her voice filled with urgency. "We need your help. The Shadow Keeper is growing stronger— his influence is spreading, and we don't know how to stop him."

The guardian's gaze shifted to Alyssa, its expression unreadable. "The Shadow Keeper is a force of great darkness, one that has threatened the balance of time for many years. His power is vast, but it is not without limits."

Kaelen felt a surge of hope at the guardian's words. "Then you can help us? You can stop him?"

The guardian's expression remained calm, but there was a hint of something—sadness, perhaps—in its eyes. "The power to stop the Shadow Keeper lies not with us, but with you, Kaelen. The gauntlet you carry is a weapon of immense power, one that can shape the very fabric of time. It is also a tool of great danger. If you are not careful, it could consume you—and all that you hold dear."

Kaelen's heart sank as the weight of the guardian's words settled over him. He had known the gauntlet was powerful, but he had never fully understood the dangers it posed—not until now.

"What do I have to do?" Kaelen asked, his voice barely above a whisper.

The guardian's gaze softened, and it stepped closer, its hand reaching out to touch Kaelen's shoulder. "You must learn to master the gauntlet, to control its power without letting it control you. Only then can you hope to stand against the Shadow Keeper."

Kaelen nodded, though the fear and doubt still gnawed at him. "How do I do that? How do I learn to control it?"

The guardian's hand tightened slightly on his shoulder; its voice gentle but firm. "You must first understand the nature of the power you wield, and the burden it carries. The gauntlet is not just a tool—it is a reflection of your own strength, your own will. To master it, you must first master yourself."

Alyssa's voice cut through the silence; her words filled with determination. "We're ready. We'll do whatever it takes."

The guardian nodded, releasing its grip on Kaelen's shoulder. "Then you shall be assessed. The sanctuary will challenge you, push you to your limits. Only by overcoming these trials can you prove yourself worthy of the gauntlet's power—and of the Time Keepers' trust."

Kaelen exchanged a glance with Alyssa, her expression filled with the same mix of determination and fear that he felt. They had come this far, faced so many challenges, but this… this was something else entirely.

There was no turning back now. The Shadow Keeper's influence was growing stronger, and time was running out. They had to find a way to stop him—no matter the cost.

The guardian stepped back, its form beginning to fade into the light. "Prepare yourselves, Kaelen Mercer, Alyssa. The trials ahead will not be easy, but they are necessary. Only by facing the darkness within can you hope to conquer the darkness without."

With those words, the guardian vanished, leaving Kaelen and Alyssa standing alone in the vast chamber. The light began to fade, the symbols on the walls dimming until the chamber was once again shrouded in shadow.

Kaelen took a deep breath, the weight of the gauntlet heavy on his back. The path ahead was uncertain, filled with dangers and trials that would assess them to their very core. They had no choice. They had to succeed.

"We'll do this together," Alyssa said, her voice steady as she reached out to take his hand. "We've come this far, Kaelen. We can't give up now."

Kaelen nodded, squeezing her hand tightly. "I know. We'll face whatever comes our way—together."

With that, they stepped forward, into the darkness, ready to face the trials that awaited them in the heart of the Time Keepers' sanctuary.

Chapter 7

The air in the sanctuary was heavy with anticipation as Kaelen and Alyssa stood before the immense doors that had opened to reveal the chamber beyond. The light from the symbols on the walls had dimmed, leaving the space in a soft, ethereal glow. The presence of the Time Keepers could be felt all around them, a silent but powerful force that seemed to observe and judge their every move.

Kaelen took a deep breath, his hand brushing against the gauntlet at his side. The artifact pulsed with a steady, rhythmic energy, its power resonating with the sanctuary itself. He could feel the connection deepening, as if the gauntlet was reaching out, seeking something within the ancient walls.

Alyssa stood beside him; her expression resolute but tinged with anxiety. They had come so far, faced so many challenges, but this—standing on the threshold of the Time Keepers' domain—felt like the culmination of everything they had endured. It was as if the entire journey had been leading to this moment.

"Are you ready?" Alyssa asked, her voice low but steady.

Kaelen nodded, though his heart raced with a mixture of fear and determination. "As ready as I'll ever be."

With that, they stepped forward, crossing the threshold into the chamber. The moment they did, the doors behind them closed with a soft, almost inaudible click, sealing them inside.

The chamber was vast, its ceiling so high that it seemed to fade into the darkness above. Pillars lined the walls, each one carved with intricate symbols and runes that glowed faintly in the dim light. The floor was smooth and polished, reflecting the light from the symbols, and the air was cool and still, as if time itself had paused within these ancient walls.

As they moved deeper into the chamber, the light began to shift, the symbols on the walls glowing brighter as if responding to their presence. The air hummed with a soft, resonant sound, growing louder with each step they took.

Then, without warning, the ground beneath them trembled, and the light flared, filling the chamber with a brilliant glow. Kaelen and Alyssa stopped, their eyes wide as they looked around, trying to understand what was happening.

From the far end of the chamber, a series of stone platforms began to rise from the floor, each one glowing with a pale blue light. The platforms were arranged in a circle, their surfaces smooth and unmarked, except for a single symbol etched into each one—a symbol that matched those on the gauntlet.

Kaelen's breath caught in his throat as he realized what he was looking at. "These are the trials," he whispered, his voice barely audible over the hum of the chamber.

Alyssa nodded, her expression serious. "We have to face them. It's the only way to prove ourselves."

Taking a deep breath, Kaelen stepped onto the first platform, feeling a surge of energy as his foot made contact with the stone. The platform flared with light, and suddenly, the world around him shifted, the sanctuary fading away as he was plunged into a new reality.

The First Trial: The Test of Will

Kaelen found himself standing in a vast, desolate landscape, the sky above him dark and stormy. The ground beneath his feet was cracked and dry, and the air was thick with the scent of sulfur and ash. The landscape was barren, devoid of life, stretching out in all directions as far as the eye could see.

He looked around, disoriented, trying to make sense of where he was. The gauntlet pulsed against his arm, its energy muted but steady, a constant reminder of the power he carried.

Then, out of the corner of his eye, he saw movement—a shadowy figure standing at the edge of his vision. He turned to face it, his heart pounding as the figure began to approach, its form becoming clearer with each step.

As the figure drew closer, Kaelen's breath caught in his throat. It was Elias.

This was not the Elias he remembered. This Elias was gaunt and hollow-eyed, his skin pale and lifeless, his clothes tattered and stained with blood. His eyes, once filled with warmth and kindness, were now cold and empty, filled with a darkness that sent chills down Kaelen's spine.

"Elias?" Kaelen whispered, his voice trembling. "Is it really you?"

The figure stopped a few feet away, its gaze fixed on Kaelen. "You failed me, Kaelen," it said, its voice a low, hollow echo. "You let me die."

Kaelen recoiled as if struck, the words cutting through him like a knife. "No… no, I didn't mean to. I tried to save you, but…"

"You failed," the figure repeated, its voice growing louder, more insistent. "And now, because of you, I am lost."

The ground beneath Kaelen's feet trembled, the cracks widening as the earth began to shift and break apart. The sky above him darkened further, the storm clouds churning with a malevolent energy.

Kaelen fell to his knees, his heart pounding in his chest. "I'm sorry, Elias. I tried… I really tried."

The figure took another step closer, its eyes burning with a cold, unforgiving light. "Your failure cost me my life, Kaelen.

And now, you carry a power that you don't understand—a power that will destroy you, just as it destroyed me."

Kaelen looked up at the figure, tears streaming down his face. "No… I won't let that happen. I won't fail again."

The figure shook its head, its expression one of pity and disdain. "You are weak, Kaelen. You are not worthy of the gauntlet. It will consume you, just as it consumed me."

Kaelen closed his eyes, the weight of the figure's words pressing down on him like a physical force. The ground beneath him continued to tremble, the cracks spreading wider, threatening to swallow him whole.

Deep within him, a spark of determination began to grow, pushing back against the darkness that threatened to overwhelm him. He had come too far, faced too many challenges, to give up now. He would not let the gauntlet consume him. He would not let his brother's memory be tainted by his own weakness.

With a deep breath, Kaelen opened his eyes, meeting the figure's cold, empty gaze. "I am not weak," he said, his voice steady. "And I will not let the gauntlet destroy me. I will master it, and I will use it to protect those I love."

The figure's expression faltered, the darkness in its eyes flickering for a moment. "You think you can control it? You think you can defy your fate?"

Kaelen stood, his resolve firm. "I don't know what the future holds, but I do know this: I will not let fear control me. I will face whatever comes my way, and I will fight for what is right."

The figure's form began to waver, the darkness around it swirling and dissipating like smoke. The cracks in the ground began to close, the storm clouds above starting to break apart, revealing patches of clear sky.

"You are stronger than I thought," the figure said, its voice fading as it began to dissolve into the air. "Remember this, Kaelen: the gauntlet is a double-edged sword. It will give you great power, but it will also demand a great price. Be prepared to pay it."

With those words, the figure vanished, leaving Kaelen alone in the desolate landscape. The ground beneath him had stopped trembling, the sky above him clearing as the storm dissipated.

Kaelen took a deep breath, the weight of the trial lifting from his shoulders. He had faced his fears, confronted the darkness within him, and emerged stronger for it. He knew that this was only the beginning. There were still more trials to face, more challenges to overcome.

And he would face them—no matter the cost.

The Second Trial: The Test of Knowledge

As the desolate landscape around him faded, Kaelen found himself standing in a new environment. He was in a vast, circular room, the walls lined with countless bookshelves that stretched up to a ceiling he could not see. The room was bathed in a soft, golden light, and the air was filled with the scent of old paper and leather.

In the center of the room stood a large, ornate table, its surface covered with scrolls, books, and various other artifacts. At the far end of the table stood a single figure, dressed in flowing robes that shimmered with the same golden light that filled the room. The figure's face was obscured by a hood, but Kaelen could feel its gaze fixed on him, observing him with a quiet intensity.

"This is the Test of Knowledge," the figure said, its voice calm and measured. "To wield the power of the gauntlet, one must understand the nature of time, the consequences of its manipulation, and the responsibilities that come with such power. Are you ready to prove your understanding?"

Kaelen nodded, though his heart raced with a mix of anticipation and apprehension. "I'm ready."

The figure gestured to the table. "Before you are three scrolls, each containing a riddle that pertains to the nature of time and the power of the gauntlet. You must solve these riddles to proceed. But be warned: failure to understand the true meaning of these riddles will result in dire consequences."

Kaelen approached the table, his eyes scanning the scrolls laid out before him. Each scroll was sealed with a wax emblem that matched the symbols on the gauntlet. Taking a deep breath, he reached for the first scroll and broke the seal, unrolling the parchment to reveal the riddle within.

The first riddle read:

"I can fly without wings. I can cry without eyes. Wherever I go, darkness follows. What am I?"

Kaelen frowned, reading the riddle several times. It was a riddle he had heard before, a classic puzzle that evaluated one's understanding of metaphor and symbolism. He thought about the answer, considering the clues carefully.

After a moment, he spoke, his voice steady. "The answer is a cloud. Clouds can move across the sky without wings, they can release rain, which could be seen as crying, and they often bring darkness with them when they cover the sun."

The figure nodded; its expression hidden but its approval evident in the softening of its posture. "You are correct. A cloud represents the transient nature of time, ever-changing and impermanent."

Kaelen felt a surge of relief as the figure gestured for him to continue. He reached for the second scroll, breaking the seal and unrolling the parchment.

The second riddle read:

"I am the beginning of everything, the end of time and space. I am essential to creation, and I surround every place. What am I?"

Kaelen's brow furrowed as he considered the riddle. This one was more abstract, challenging his understanding of both language and the concepts of time and space. He thought about the clues, letting the words roll over in his mind.

Finally, he spoke. "The answer is the letter 'E.' It is the first letter of the word 'everything,' the last letter in the words 'time' and 'space,' and it is found in the words 'creation' and 'place.'"

The figure nodded once more. "Correct. The letter 'E' is a reminder of the constants that exist even within the vastness of time and space."

Kaelen felt another wave of relief, though he knew the final riddle would likely be the most difficult. He reached for the third scroll, his heart pounding as he broke the seal and unrolled the parchment.

The third riddle read:

"To move forward, you must first go back. To gain, you must lose. To win, you must accept defeat. What am I?"

Kaelen's mind raced as he considered the riddle. This one was different from the others, more philosophical in nature. It spoke to the paradoxes inherent in the manipulation of time and the responsibilities that came with wielding such power.

He thought about the trials he had faced so far, the lessons he had learned along the way. The riddle was not just about time, but about the nature of sacrifice, the balance of power, and the consequences of one's actions.

"The answer..." Kaelen began, hesitating as he considered his response. "The answer is time itself. Time is a paradox, a force that requires balance and understanding. To move forward in time, one must often look to the past. To gain something, one must be willing to sacrifice something else. And to truly win, one must accept the possibility of failure."

The figure was silent for a long moment, its gaze fixed on Kaelen. Then, slowly, it nodded. "You have understood the lesson. Time is not just a force to be wielded—it is a responsibility, one that requires wisdom, humility, and understanding."

Kaelen let out a breath he hadn't realized he was holding, the tension in his body easing as the figure stepped back, allowing him to pass.

"You have proven your knowledge," the figure said, its voice filled with a quiet respect. "There is still one more trial you must face before you can claim the gauntlet's true power."

The Third Trial: The Test of Sacrifice

Kaelen stepped forward, the walls of the circular room dissolving into mist as the scene around him changed once again. He found himself standing in a vast, open field, the sky above clear and bright. The air was warm, filled with the scent of wildflowers and fresh grass.

Despite the peaceful surroundings, Kaelen felt a deep sense of unease. He could sense the final trial approaching, the weight of it pressing down on him like a heavy burden.

As he walked forward, the field around him began to shift, the grass parting to reveal a narrow path that led to a distant figure standing alone in the center of the field. The figure was turned away from him, but Kaelen recognized it at once—Alyssa.

His heart leaped into his throat as he began to run toward her, calling out her name. As he approached, the ground beneath him began to tremble, cracks forming in the earth, widening into deep chasms that separated him from Alyssa.

"Alyssa!" Kaelen shouted; his voice filled with desperation. "Hold on, I'm coming!"

Alyssa didn't respond. She remained motionless, her gaze fixed on something in the distance, as if unaware of the danger that surrounded her.

Kaelen pushed forward, leaping over the widening chasms, his heart pounding with fear. No matter how hard he tried, the distance between them seemed to grow, the ground continuing to crack and split beneath his feet.

Finally, he reached the edge of a particularly wide chasm, the gap too vast to jump. He skidded to a halt, his breath coming in ragged gasps as he looked at Alyssa, who stood on the other side, still oblivious to his presence.

"Alyssa, please!" Kaelen cried out, his voice breaking. "I'm here! I'm right here!"

Alyssa didn't turn, her gaze still fixed on something beyond the horizon.

Kaelen's heart ached with desperation as he looked down at the chasm, the darkness within it seeming to stretch on forever. He knew he couldn't reach her—not like this. The distance was too great, the gap too wide.

And then he heard a voice, soft and whispering, echoing in the back of his mind. It was the voice of the figure from his first trial, the one that had taken the form of Elias.

"You must choose, Kaelen," the voice whispered. "You must choose between the gauntlet and the one you love. To gain the power to protect the future, you must be willing to sacrifice the present."

Kaelen shook his head, tears streaming down his face. "No… no, I can't. I can't choose."

"You must," the voice insisted, growing louder, more insistent. "The gauntlet demands a price, Kaelen. Are you willing to pay it?"

Kaelen looked up at Alyssa, his heart breaking as he realized what the trial was asking of him. He could see her now, so clearly, her face filled with determination, her eyes shining with hope. She was the one who had stood by him through everything, the one who had believed in him even when he had doubted himself.

The gauntlet was more than just a weapon—it was a tool that could shape the future, protect those who could not protect themselves. It was the key to stopping the Shadow Keeper, to ensuring that time itself did not fall into darkness.

Kaelen's hands trembled as he reached for the gauntlet, the weight of his decision pressing down on him like a crushing force. He knew what he had to do, but the thought of losing Alyssa, of sacrificing the one person who meant everything to him, was unbearable.

"I'm sorry," Kaelen whispered, his voice choked with emotion. "I'm so sorry."

With a deep breath, Kaelen closed his eyes, focusing on the gauntlet, on the power it held. He could feel its energy pulsing through him, resonating with his very soul.

And then, with a final, heart-wrenching decision, Kaelen activated the gauntlet, channeling its power into the chasm before him.

The ground trembled as the gauntlet's energy surged through the earth, closing the chasm, sealing the cracks. As the power faded, Kaelen felt a deep, aching emptiness in his chest—a void where Alyssa's presence had once been.

When he opened his eyes, the field was gone, replaced by the empty, echoing chamber of the sanctuary. The trial was over, but the cost had been high.

Kaelen fell to his knees, his heart heavy with the weight of his sacrifice. He had passed the trial, but at what cost? The gauntlet's power was his, but it had demanded a price he wasn't sure he could bear.

As the chamber settled into silence, the light in the room began to shift, softening into a warm, golden glow. The air hummed with energy, and from the far end of the chamber, a series of figures began to materialize.

The Time Keepers had arrived.

Kaelen looked up, his breath catching in his throat as the figures took shape before him. There were five of them, each one distinct, yet all sharing an air of ancient wisdom and immense power. Their forms were ethereal, almost translucent, their robes shimmering with the same golden light that filled the chamber.

"Kaelen Mercer," one of the Time Keepers said, its voice calm and resonant. "You have faced the trials of the sanctuary and proven yourself worthy of the gauntlet's power."

Kaelen nodded, though his heart was still heavy with the weight of his recent sacrifice. "I… I did what I had to do."

The Time Keeper stepped forward, its gaze fixed on Kaelen with a mixture of respect and sadness. "The path you have chosen is not an easy one. The gauntlet is a tool of great power, but it is also a burden. It will demand sacrifices, and the decisions you make will shape the very fabric of time."

Kaelen swallowed hard, the words cutting through him like a blade. "I understand."

Another of the Time Keepers stepped forward, its voice soft but firm. "The gauntlet was created long ago, forged by those who sought to protect time from those who would seek to corrupt it. It is a weapon, yes, but it is also a shield—a tool to preserve the balance of time."

"The Shadow Keeper seeks to use the gauntlet for his own purposes," another Time Keeper said, its voice filled with a quiet intensity. "He wishes to reshape time in his image, to bend it to his will. If he succeeds, the consequences will be catastrophic."

Kaelen nodded, his resolve hardening. "I won't let that happen. I'll stop him."

The Time Keepers exchanged a glance, their expressions grave. "The task before you are great, Kaelen Mercer. The Shadow Keeper is powerful, and he will stop at nothing to achieve his goals. You are not alone in this fight."

Kaelen looked up, hope flickering in his chest. "You'll help me?"

The Time Keeper who had spoken first nodded. "We will guide you, Kaelen. The path you must walk is yours alone. The gauntlet is a tool, but it is your heart, your will, which will decide the outcome of this battle."

Kaelen felt a surge of determination, the weight of his mission settling over him like a mantle. He had faced the trials, proven his worth, and now he understood the gravity of the task before him.

The fate of time itself rested in his hands.

"We believe in you, Kaelen," one of the Time Keepers said, its voice filled with quiet strength. "You have the power to protect the future, to ensure that time remains unbroken. You must be prepared to make the hardest choices, to face the darkest challenges."

Kaelen nodded, his heart steady. "I'm ready."

The Time Keepers stepped back, their forms beginning to fade into the golden light. "Then go, Kaelen Mercer. The gauntlet is yours. Use it wisely and remember that the choices you make will echo through eternity."

With those words, the Time Keepers vanished, leaving Kaelen alone in the chamber. The light slowly faded, the symbols on the walls dimming until the room was once again shrouded in shadow.

Kaelen stood, the weight of the gauntlet heavy on his arm, but the resolve in his heart stronger than ever. He had passed the trials, gained the power of the gauntlet, and now, he understood the responsibility that came with it.

The road ahead would be difficult, filled with danger and sacrifice, but Kaelen was ready. He would face whatever challenges lay ahead, fight against the Shadow Keeper, and protect the future from those who sought to destroy it.

For Elias, for Alyssa, for the future—he would not fail.

With a deep breath, Kaelen turned and walked out of the chamber, the weight of his mission pressing down on him, but the strength in his heart carrying him forward.

Chapter 8

The soft golden light of the sanctuary's inner chamber began to fade as Kaelen and Alyssa made their way out, the weight of the Time Keepers' words heavy on their shoulders. The ancient beings had imparted knowledge, wisdom, and a burden that Kaelen now felt keenly as they descended back into the dense forest that shrouded the hidden sanctuary.

The air was cool, the leaves above rustling softly in the breeze as if whispering secrets of the ancient forest. As the doors of the sanctuary closed behind them with a resonant thud, sealing the secrets within, Kaelen couldn't help but feel a pang of uncertainty. The gauntlet on his arm was now more than just an artifact—it was a symbol of his new responsibility and the immense power he had to master.

Alyssa walked beside him in silence, her gaze focused ahead, though Kaelen could tell she was deep in thought. The trials they had faced in the sanctuary had tested them both, pushing them to the brink of their endurance, and revealing truths about themselves that were both sobering and necessary.

As they moved away from the sanctuary, the dense forest began to open up, revealing a narrow path that wound through the trees. The sun was setting, casting long shadows across the ground, and the air was filled with the scent of pine and earth.

Kaelen finally broke the silence, his voice quiet but determined. "We've come so far, but I know the hardest part is still ahead."

Alyssa nodded, her expression serious. "The Time Keepers warned us about the dangers of the gauntlet, but they also gave us hope. We have the power to stop the Shadow Keeper, but it won't be easy. We have to be ready for anything."

Kaelen looked down at the gauntlet, the intricate symbols etched into its surface glowing faintly in the dim light. He could feel its power coursing through him, a steady, rhythmic pulse that resonated with his very being. Along with that power came a deep sense of responsibility—a weight that pressed down on him like a heavy mantle.

"We need to keep moving," Kaelen said, his voice firm. "The Shadow Keeper won't wait for us to be ready. We have to use the time we have wisely."

Alyssa agreed, and they continued down the path, their footsteps silent on the forest floor. As they walked, Kaelen began to focus on the gauntlet, trying to sense its power and understand how to control it. He knew that mastering the gauntlet was crucial if they were to succeed in their mission, and the Time Keepers had made it clear that this was no small task.

After a while, Kaelen stopped and turned to Alyssa. "I need to practice—now. The Time Keepers warned me that the gauntlet's power can be unpredictable. I need to learn how to control it, to use it when we need it most."

Alyssa nodded, understanding the urgency. "I'll keep watch. We can't afford to be caught off guard."

Kaelen found a small clearing off the path, a space where he could focus without distraction. He took a deep breath and closed his eyes, letting the sounds of the forest fade into the background as he reached out with his senses, feeling the energy of the gauntlet.

The power within the gauntlet was immense, like a vast reservoir of energy just waiting to be tapped. It was also wild, untamed, and Kaelen knew that controlling it would require more than just willpower—it would require understanding, patience, and finesse.

He began with something simple, focusing on slowing down time around him. He could feel the energy within the gauntlet responding to his intent, but as he tried to direct it, the power surged, nearly slipping out of his control. The world around him seemed to blur, the movement of the leaves slowing to a crawl, but the strain of holding the power was immense.

Kaelen gritted his teeth, forcing himself to maintain control. He could feel the gauntlet pushing back, resisting his attempts to command it, but he didn't back down. He needed to master this—he had to.

Slowly, the power began to stabilize, the world around him settling into a slow-motion rhythm. The leaves drifted lazily through the air, and the sound of the wind became a low, drawn-out hum. Kaelen held the effect for a few moments, feeling the strain in his mind and body, before finally releasing the power and allowing time to return to its normal flow.

He staggered slightly, the effort leaving him momentarily drained. Despite the difficulty, he felt a surge of satisfaction. He had done it—he had controlled the gauntlet's power, if only for a brief moment.

Alyssa was at his side in an instant, her eyes filled with concern. "Are you alright?"

Kaelen nodded, though his breath came in short gasps. "I'm fine... just need to catch my breath."

She helped him sit down on a fallen log, her expression serious. "You need to be careful, Kaelen. The gauntlet's power is incredible, but it's also dangerous. You can't push yourself too hard."

Kaelen nodded, appreciating her concern. "I know. But we don't have much time. I have to learn how to use this power if we're going to have any chance of stopping the Shadow Keeper."

Alyssa placed a hand on his shoulder, her touch grounding him. "We'll figure it out together. Just remember, you don't have to do this alone."

Kaelen smiled, the warmth of her words giving him strength. "I couldn't do this without you, Alyssa."

They rested for a while, Kaelen regaining his strength as the light of the setting sun cast long shadows across the clearing. The forest was quiet, the only sound the gentle rustle of leaves in the breeze. Even in this moment of peace, Kaelen could feel the urgency of their mission pressing down on him. The Shadow Keeper was out there, growing stronger with each passing day, and they couldn't afford to waste any time.

After a while, they continued on their journey, the path leading them deeper into the forest. Kaelen kept practicing with the gauntlet as they walked, focusing on simple exercises—slowing time, speeding it up, even attempting to heal a small cut on his hand. Each time, the gauntlet responded, but it was clear that controlling its power was a delicate balance. Too much force, and the power would slip out of his grasp; too little, and the gauntlet would refuse to respond at all.

As night fell, they decided to set up camp, choosing a small, secluded area near a stream. The sound of the water was soothing, and the soft glow of the moonlight filtering through the trees provided just enough light for them to see by.

Kaelen sat by the fire, the warmth of the flames a welcome comfort in the cool night air. Alyssa sat across from him, her eyes reflecting the flickering light as she watched him with a thoughtful expression.

"You're doing well," she said after a while, breaking the silence. "I can see you're starting to get the hang of it."

Kaelen nodded, though he still felt the weight of the challenges ahead. "It's not easy. The power is… overwhelming. However I'm starting to understand how it works, how to control it. I just need more practice."

Alyssa smiled, a glint of pride in her eyes. "You're stronger than you think, Kaelen. The Time Keepers chose you for a reason."

Kaelen looked down at the gauntlet, the symbols etched into its surface glowing faintly in the firelight. "I just hope I can live up to their expectations."

"You will," Alyssa said firmly. "I believe in you."

Kaelen met her gaze, the sincerity in her words filling him with a renewed sense of determination. He had come so far, faced so many challenges, and now, with Alyssa by his side, he knew he could face whatever lay ahead.

They settled down to sleep, the fire crackling softly as the night deepened around them. Even as he closed his eyes, Kaelen couldn't shake the feeling that something was wrong—that the gauntlet's power was drawing them closer to something dangerous, something they weren't yet prepared to face.

The next morning, they broke camp and continued on their journey, the forest gradually giving way to rolling hills and open fields. The air was crisp and cool, the sky a clear, brilliant blue. Despite the beauty of the landscape, Kaelen couldn't shake the sense of unease that had settled over him like a shadow.

As they crested a hill, they came across a small village nestled in the valley below. Smoke rose from the chimneys, and the sound of voices and laughter carried on the breeze, a stark contrast to the tension Kaelen felt within.

As they approached the village, it quickly became clear that something was very wrong. The air grew thick with an unnatural stillness, and the light around them seemed to flicker and warp, as if time itself was being twisted and bent.

Kaelen slowed his pace, his hand instinctively going to the gauntlet. "Do you feel that?"

Alyssa nodded, her eyes scanning the village with growing concern. "Something's not right. The Time Keepers warned us about temporal anomalies… this must be one of them."

As they entered the village, the sense of wrongness intensified. The people they passed seemed to move in slow motion, their actions sluggish and distorted, as if they were caught in a time loop. Some stood frozen in place, their faces contorted in expressions of fear and confusion.

Kaelen's heart pounded in his chest as he tried to make sense of what he was seeing. "This is the Shadow Keeper's doing. His influence is spreading—he's disrupting time itself."

They moved cautiously through the village, trying to avoid drawing attention to themselves. It was clear that the anomaly was growing more severe. Buildings flickered in and out of existence, the landscape around them shifting and changing in ways that defied logic.

"We need to do something," Alyssa said urgently. "If we don't fix this, the entire village could be lost."

Kaelen nodded, though the weight of the task ahead filled him with dread. He knew that using the gauntlet to fix the anomaly would be dangerous—he could easily make things worse if he wasn't careful. He also knew that they couldn't leave the village like this, trapped in a distorted version of time.

He took a deep breath, focusing on the gauntlet and the power within. "I'll try to stabilize the anomaly, but I need to be careful. The Time Keepers warned me about the dangers of altering time."

Alyssa placed a reassuring hand on his arm. "I trust you, Kaelen. Just take it slow—we'll figure this out together."

Kaelen nodded, feeling a surge of determination. He closed his eyes, reaching out with his senses, trying to feel the flow of time around him. The gauntlet responded, its power flaring to life, resonating with the chaotic energy of the anomaly.

He began by slowing down time, focusing on a small area around him. The air seemed to thicken, the sounds around him fading into a low hum as time itself slowed to a crawl. The flickering images of the village steadied, the shifting landscape stabilizing as Kaelen carefully manipulated the flow of time.

As he worked, he could feel the strain of the gauntlet's power, the wild, untamed energy pushing back against his control. The more he tried to fix the anomaly, the more it resisted, the temporal distortions growing stronger, more unpredictable.

Kaelen gritted his teeth, forcing himself to maintain focus. He could feel the gauntlet's power slipping, the energy threatening to spiral out of control. He couldn't stop—not now, not when the village was at stake.

"Kaelen, be careful!" Alyssa's voice cut through the tension, grounding him. "You're pushing too hard!"

He knew she was right, but he couldn't afford to back down. The anomaly was too severe—if he didn't fix it now, the consequences could be disastrous.

Then, as he reached the limit of his endurance, Kaelen sensed something—a shift in the flow of time, a ripple in the fabric of reality. The anomaly was reacting to his attempts to stabilize it, but not in the way he had hoped. The temporal distortions were converging, building into a massive surge of energy that threatened to tear the village apart.

Kaelen's heart raced as he realized the gravity of the situation. If he continued to push, he could cause a catastrophic collapse of time in the area, trapping the villagers in an endless loop—or worse, erasing them from existence entirely.

He had to make a choice: risk everything to fix the anomaly or pull back and leave the village to its fate.

It was an impossible decision, one that weighed heavily on him as he struggled to maintain control. The gauntlet's power surged, the energy within it growing more volatile by the second.

"Alyssa, I... I don't know what to do," Kaelen admitted, his voice strained with the effort of holding the power at bay.

Alyssa stepped closer; her expression filled with determination. "We can't let the village be destroyed, Kaelen. But you also can't push yourself too far. Maybe... maybe there's another way."

Kaelen looked at her, desperation in his eyes. "What other way? The Time Keepers warned me about the risks of altering time, and now… now I'm not sure I can fix this without causing more harm."

Alyssa's gaze was steady, her voice calm but firm. "Kaelen, you don't have to do this alone. Let me help you—together, we can find a solution."

Her words brought a sense of clarity, cutting through the chaos in Kaelen's mind. He realized that she was right—they were in this together, and he didn't have to bear the burden alone.

Taking a deep breath, Kaelen refocused his efforts, this time drawing on Alyssa's strength and support. He shifted his approach, instead of trying to force the anomaly back into place, he began to work with the flow of time, gently guiding the distortions into a more stable pattern.

It was slow, painstaking work, but gradually, the chaos began to subside. The flickering images steadied, the landscape around them returning to something resembling normalcy. The villagers, who had been trapped in time loops, began to move again, their actions returning to a natural pace.

Kaelen felt the strain of the gauntlet's power lessen, the wild energy settling into a more manageable flow. The anomaly wasn't fully fixed, but it was stabilized—for now.

He let out a long breath, his body trembling with exhaustion as he released the last of the gauntlet's power. The village was safe, but the effort had taken its toll.

Alyssa was at his side, supporting him as he struggled to stay on his feet. "You did it, Kaelen. The village is safe."

Kaelen nodded, though his heart was heavy with the knowledge of what could have happened. "I almost lost control... I could have made things worse."

"But you didn't," Alyssa said firmly. "You found a way, Kaelen. You worked with the gauntlet, not against it. That's how you're going to win—by staying true to yourself and to those who believe in you."

Kaelen looked at her, the sincerity in her eyes filling him with a renewed sense of purpose. She was right—he had found a way to stabilize the anomaly, but more importantly, he had done it by trusting in his own abilities and in the bond, he shared with Alyssa.

As they left the village behind, Kaelen knew that the challenges ahead would only grow more difficult. The Shadow Keeper's influence was spreading, and time itself was in danger.

He also knew that he wasn't alone—that with Alyssa by his side, he could face whatever came their way.

As the day wore on, they continued their journey, the landscape gradually changing from rolling hills to rugged, mountainous terrain. The air grew cooler, the sky a deeper shade of blue as they ascended into the higher elevations.

Kaelen could feel the weight of the gauntlet more acutely now, the strain of using its power taking a toll on his body and mind. He also felt a growing sense of determination—a resolve to master the gauntlet, to use it to protect the future and stop the Shadow Keeper from plunging the world into darkness.

As they reached the crest of a mountain ridge, Kaelen suddenly felt a sharp, searing pain in his head. He staggered, clutching his temple as a wave of dizziness washed over him.

"Kaelen!" Alyssa was at his side in an instant, her voice filled with concern. "What's wrong?"

Kaelen tried to speak, but the words caught in his throat as a vision overtook him—a vision so intense, so vivid, that it felt as if he were being pulled out of his own body.

He saw a figure, tall and imposing, shrouded in shadow. The figure's eyes burned with a malevolent light, and the air around him crackled with dark energy. Kaelen recognized the figure immediately—it was the Shadow Keeper.

The vision shifted, showing scenes of devastation: cities in ruins, the sky darkened by unnatural storms, the very fabric of time unraveling as the Shadow Keeper's power spread across the land.

And then, the vision focused on Kaelen himself. He saw himself standing alone, the gauntlet on his arm glowing with an ominous light. He was surrounded by the twisted remains of a battlefield, the bodies of those he had failed to protect lying at his feet. The Shadow Keeper loomed over him, his voice a low, mocking whisper that echoed in Kaelen's mind.

"You are too late, Kaelen Mercer. Time belongs to me."

With a jolt, Kaelen was pulled back to reality, the vision fading as quickly as it had come. He gasped for breath, his heart racing as the terror of what he had seen lingered in his mind.

Alyssa held him steady, her eyes wide with worry. "Kaelen, what happened? What did you see?"

Kaelen swallowed hard, trying to shake off the lingering fear. "It was him... the Shadow Keeper. He's growing stronger, Alyssa. I saw... I saw what he's planning, what he's going to do if we don't stop him."

Alyssa's expression hardened, her resolve as strong as ever. "Then we'll stop him. Whatever it takes, we'll find a way."

Kaelen nodded, though the vision had shaken him to his core. The Shadow Keeper was more powerful than he had imagined, and the stakes were higher than ever. He couldn't let fear control him—he had to stay focused, to use the gauntlet's power for good, to protect those who couldn't protect themselves.

As they continued their journey, Kaelen couldn't shake the feeling that the vision was more than just a warning—it was a glimpse of the future that awaited them if they failed.

No matter what lay ahead, Kaelen knew one thing for certain: he would not let the Shadow Keeper win. He would fight with everything he had, and he would protect the future, no matter the cost.

For Elias, for Alyssa, for the world—they would find a way.

Chapter 9

The air was thin and crisp as Kaelen and Alyssa climbed the narrow path that wound its way through the rugged mountains. The late afternoon sun cast long shadows across the rocky terrain, but the beauty of the landscape was lost on them. Their minds were focused on the task at hand—finding the Nexus Shrine and uncovering the secrets it held.

The Nexus Shrine was an ancient place, hidden deep within the mountains and protected by powerful wards and temporal anomalies. According to the information they had gathered, the shrine was the last known location of the Nexus Crystal, a powerful artifact tied to the flow of time itself. Kaelen could feel the energy of the Nexus through the gauntlet, a steady, rhythmic pulse that seemed to grow stronger the closer they got.

Something felt off. The closer they came to the shrine, the more Kaelen sensed that something was missing—something vital. The Nexus Crystal should have been radiating an immense power, but instead, there was only a faint echo, as if the crystal's presence had been erased or hidden.

Alyssa noticed his unease. "What's wrong?"

Kaelen shook his head, trying to focus. "I'm not sure. I can feel the Nexus, but it's faint—like it's not fully there. The crystal should be radiating power, but all I'm sensing is a shadow of what it should be."

Alyssa frowned, her eyes scanning the path ahead. "Do you think the crystal is gone?"

Kaelen didn't answer immediately. He had considered the possibility, but it was a thought too troubling to fully embrace. If the Nexus Crystal was missing, their mission would become infinitely more complicated. The crystal was key to maintaining the stability of the timeline—without it, the very fabric of time could begin to unravel.

"We'll know soon enough," Kaelen finally said, his voice grim. "Let's keep moving."

They continued their ascent, the path growing steeper and more treacherous as they climbed. The mountain was unforgiving, the jagged rocks and loose gravel making every step a calculated risk. Kaelen and Alyssa pressed on, driven by the urgency of their mission and the knowledge that time was running out.

As they rounded a bend, the entrance to the Nexus Shrine came into view. The shrine was built into the side of the mountain, its entrance marked by a massive stone archway adorned with ancient symbols and runes. The air around the entrance shimmered with a faint, ethereal light, a sign of the powerful wards that protected the shrine from intruders.

Kaelen could feel the energy of the wards, a tingling sensation that brushed against his skin as they approached. The gauntlet responded to the presence of the Nexus, its power resonating with the wards as if recognizing a kindred force.

"This is it," Kaelen said, his voice low as they stood before the archway. "The Nexus Shrine."

Alyssa stepped forward, her eyes narrowing as she examined the symbols etched into the stone. "These runes... they're incredibly old. Whoever built this place went to great lengths to protect it."

Kaelen nodded; his gaze fixed on the entrance. "The Nexus Crystal is one of the most powerful artifacts in existence. It makes sense that they would want to keep it safe."

They exchanged a glance, both understanding the gravity of what lay ahead. If the crystal was indeed missing, they would need to uncover its whereabouts quickly, before the Shadow Keeper could get his hands on it.

With a deep breath, Kaelen stepped forward, his hand brushing against the cold stone of the archway. The moment he made contact, the runes flared to life, glowing with a brilliant light that filled the air with a soft hum.

The entrance to the shrine began to open, the massive stone doors grinding apart with a deep, resonant rumble that echoed through the mountains. Kaelen and Alyssa tensed, ready for whatever might await them inside.

As the doors fully opened, they were met with a blast of cold air, the interior of the shrine shrouded in shadow. The light from the runes illuminated the entrance, revealing a long, narrow corridor that seemed to stretch on endlessly into the darkness.

Kaelen felt a shiver run down his spine as he peered into the gloom. The energy of the Nexus was stronger now, but it was still faint—an echo of what it should have been.

"This place feels… off," Alyssa said, her voice barely above a whisper.

Kaelen nodded; his gaze focused on the corridor ahead. "We need to be careful. The Nexus Shrine is likely filled with traps and puzzles designed to protect the crystal."

Together, they stepped into the corridor, their footsteps echoing softly on the stone floor. The air inside the shrine was cold and still, the silence oppressive. The walls were lined with more symbols and runes, their faint glow providing just enough light to see by.

As they moved deeper into the shrine, the corridor began to branch off into a series of smaller passages, each one leading to a different chamber. Kaelen could feel the energy of the Nexus growing stronger with each step, but it was still fragmented, as if something was blocking its full power.

They chose a passage at random, following it to a large chamber filled with intricate carvings and statues. The chamber was dominated by a massive stone pedestal in the center, its surface etched with more symbols and runes.

"This must be one of the main chambers," Alyssa said as she approached the pedestal. "Look at the carvings—they depict scenes from different points in time."

Kaelen examined the carvings, his brow furrowing as he recognized the scenes. "These are moments of great importance—events that shaped the course of history. It's like a record of time itself."

Alyssa ran her fingers over the symbols on the pedestal, her expression thoughtful. "These symbols... they're similar to the ones on the gauntlet. I think this pedestal was used to channel the power of the Nexus Crystal."

Kaelen stepped closer, his eyes narrowing as he studied the pedestal. "But the crystal is missing. Without it, the pedestal is just a relic."

Alyssa nodded, her gaze turning to the inscriptions carved into the pedestal's base. "There's something written here... it looks like a warning."

Kaelen knelt beside her, reading the ancient text. The language was old, but he could make out the general meaning: "The crystal is the keystone. Without it, time will falter. It has been hidden, taken from the Nexus to protect the flow of time. Only those who understand the path may find it."

Kaelen's heart sank as he read the words. "The crystal isn't here. It's been taken, hidden somewhere in the world—and in time."

Alyssa looked up at him, her expression filled with concern. "If the crystal was taken out of the Nexus, it could be anywhere... any when. How are we supposed to find it?"

Kaelen didn't have an answer. The task before them seemed impossible finding a single artifact hidden somewhere in the vast expanse of time. They didn't have a choice. Without the Nexus Crystal, the stability of the timeline was at risk, and the Shadow Keeper would stop at nothing to find it and bend time to his will.

"We'll have to follow the clues," Kaelen said, his voice determined. "There must be more information here—something that can point us in the right direction."

Alyssa nodded, though the worry in her eyes was clear. "We need to hurry. If the Shadow Keeper finds out the crystal is missing, he'll come after it too."

They continued their exploration of the shrine, moving from chamber to chamber in search of more clues. The shrine was a labyrinth of passages and rooms, each one filled with ancient artifacts and inscriptions that hinted at the history of the Nexus and its role in protecting the timeline.

In one chamber, they found a series of murals depicting the creation of the Nexus Crystal. The images showed a group of ancient beings—possibly the first Time Keepers—harnessing the raw energy of time itself to forge the crystal, imbuing it with the power to stabilize and protect the timeline.

"The Nexus Crystal was created to be the anchor of time," Alyssa said, studying the murals. "It's what keeps the flow of time stable, preventing any one person or event from disrupting the entire timeline."

Kaelen nodded, his mind racing as he tried to piece together the puzzle. "If the crystal is missing, that stability is at risk. The Shadow Keeper could use that instability to manipulate time, to reshape reality according to his will."

They found more inscriptions in another chamber, these ones detailing the process of hiding the crystal. The text spoke of a great threat that arose, forcing the Time Keepers to remove the crystal from the Nexus and hide it somewhere in the real world, embedding it within a specific moment in time to keep it safe.

"The crystal was hidden to protect it," Kaelen said, reading the inscriptions aloud. "The process was dangerous—it involved manipulating time itself to place the crystal in a moment where it couldn't be easily found."

Alyssa frowned, her eyes narrowing as she considered the implications. "But that means... if we want to find the crystal, we'll need to track down the exact moment in time where it was hidden. We'll need to understand the path they took."

Kaelen felt a surge of determination. "We can do it. The gauntlet can help us—if we can figure out how to use it to trace the crystal's path."

As they continued searching the shrine, they found more clues—fragmented pieces of information that hinted at the crystal's location. The more they uncovered, the more they realized how difficult their task would be. The Nexus Crystal had been hidden with great care, and the clues were scattered, each one leading to another piece of the puzzle.

Just as they were piecing together a potential lead, Kaelen felt a sudden surge of dark energy—a wave of malevolent power that sent a chill down his spine. He turned to Alyssa, his expression grim. "We're not alone."

Alyssa's eyes widened as she sensed it too. "The Shadow Keeper?"

Kaelen nodded, his hand instinctively going to the gauntlet. "Or his minions. We need to be ready."

No sooner had the words left his mouth than the entrance to the chamber exploded in a burst of dark energy, the shockwave sending them both sprawling to the ground. Kaelen scrambled to his feet, his heart pounding as he saw a group of figures emerge from the smoke and debris.

The Legion of Shadows. A group of rogue time travelers, each one corrupted by the Shadow Keeper's influence. They were led by a tall, imposing figure clad in dark armor, his face hidden behind a mask that glowed with a sickly green light—the Shadow Keeper's lieutenant, known only as the Shadow Keeper.

The Time Keeper

"Kaelen Mercer," the Shadow Keeper intoned, his voice echoing through the chamber. "You've come far, but your journey ends here."

Kaelen tightened his grip on the gauntlet, his mind racing as he assessed the situation. They were outnumbered, and the Legion of Shadows was a formidable foe. They had no choice— they had to fight.

"Alyssa, stay close," Kaelen said, his voice tense. "We need to get out of here with the information we've gathered."

Alyssa nodded; her expression steely as she drew her weapon. "We can't let them stop us."

The Shadow Keeper's lieutenant raised his hand, and the Legion of Shadows advanced, their movements fluid and unnaturally fast. Kaelen felt the gauntlet's power surge in response, the energy crackling around him as he prepared to defend them.

The battle was fierce and chaotic, the chamber filled with the sounds of clashing weapons and the hum of temporal energy. Kaelen used the gauntlet to slow time around them, giving them a brief advantage as they fought their way toward the exit. The

145

Legion was relentless, their attacks coordinated and precise, forcing Kaelen to push the gauntlet to its limits.

At one point, Kaelen was nearly overwhelmed, the Shadow Keeper's lieutenant bearing down on him with a blade wreathed in dark energy. Alyssa was there, her quick thinking and agility allowing her to strike the lieutenant from behind, giving Kaelen the opening he needed to drive him back.

"We can't keep this up," Alyssa shouted over the din of battle. "We need to get out of here!"

Kaelen knew she was right. The Legion was too powerful, and they couldn't afford to be caught here. With a final burst of energy, Kaelen created a temporal distortion, throwing the Legion off balance and giving them a brief window to escape.

"Now!" Kaelen yelled, grabbing Alyssa's hand as they sprinted for the exit.

They raced through the corridors, the sounds of battle and the shouts of the Legion fading behind them. The shrine was a labyrinth, but Kaelen's sense of direction was sharp, guided by the gauntlet and the urgency of their mission.

As they burst through the entrance and into the open air, Kaelen felt the cold mountain wind hit his face, a stark contrast to the stifling atmosphere inside the shrine. There was no time to rest—they had to keep moving.

"We have to lose them in the mountains," Kaelen said, his breath coming in ragged gasps. "They'll be right behind us."

Alyssa nodded, and they set off down the mountain path, their pace frantic as they put as much distance as possible between themselves and the Nexus Shrine.

The journey down the mountain was treacherous, the rocky terrain and steep slopes making every step a challenge. Kaelen and Alyssa pressed on, driven by the knowledge that the Legion of Shadows was on their heels.

After what felt like hours, they finally reached a sheltered valley, the dense forest providing them with some cover. Exhausted and battered, they found a small cave where they could take refuge and catch their breath.

Kaelen collapsed against the wall of the cave, his body aching from the battle and the strain of using the gauntlet. Alyssa sat beside him, her face streaked with dirt and sweat, but her eyes were bright with determination.

"We did it," she said, her voice filled with a mixture of relief and resolve. "We got out with the clues."

Kaelen nodded, though the weight of their mission still pressed heavily on his mind. "But we're not done yet. The crystal is still out there, and the Shadow Keeper will be hunting for it."

Alyssa placed a hand on his arm, her touch grounding him. "We'll find it, Kaelen. We're closer now—we just need to follow the clues."

Kaelen looked at her, the sincerity in her words giving him strength. They had faced overwhelming odds and emerged with the knowledge they needed to continue their quest. The Nexus Crystal was still out there, hidden somewhere in time, and they were one step closer to finding it.

As they rested in the cave, Kaelen allowed himself a moment of hope. The journey ahead would be long and dangerous, but he wasn't alone. With Alyssa by his side and the gauntlet's power in his hands, he knew they had a fighting chance.

For the first time since they had entered the Nexus Shrine, Kaelen felt a glimmer of optimism. The crystal might be hidden, but it wasn't lost. They would find it—and they would stop the Shadow Keeper before he could plunge the world into darkness.

The battle for the future was far from over, but Kaelen was ready. Together, they would protect the timeline and ensure that the Nexus Crystal returned to its rightful place.

With a deep breath, Kaelen leaned back against the wall of the cave, his resolve solidifying. The path ahead was uncertain, but one thing was clear: they would not stop until the Nexus Crystal was found, and the Shadow Keeper's plans were thwarted.

And no matter what challenges lay ahead, Kaelen knew they would face them together.

Chapter 10

Kaelen and Alyssa raced through the dense forest, the cold mountain air burning in their lungs as they pushed themselves to their limits. The trees were a blur around them, the sounds of their footsteps muffled by the thick undergrowth. The memory of the Nexus Shrine, the battle with the Legion of Shadows, and the narrow escape was still fresh in their minds, driving them to move faster, to stay ahead of the danger that pursued them.

Kaelen's heart pounded in his chest; each beat a reminder of the relentless pace they had been keeping since leaving the shrine. His muscles burned with exhaustion, but he knew they couldn't stop—not yet. The gauntlet on his arm pulsed with a steady, rhythmic energy, its power a constant reminder of the responsibility he carried. The weight of that responsibility also made him acutely aware of the dangers they faced.

Beside him, Alyssa moved with a grace and determination that belied her own fatigue. She was silent, her focus entirely on the path ahead, but Kaelen could see the strain in her eyes. They were both running on borrowed time, and they knew it.

"We need to find somewhere to rest," Kaelen said, his voice strained but urgent. "We can't keep this pace up forever."

Alyssa nodded, though her expression remained tense. "There's a clearing up ahead. We'll take a moment to regroup."

They continued through the forest, the trees gradually thinning as they approached the clearing Alyssa had mentioned. When they finally emerged from the cover of the trees, they found themselves in a small, open space surrounded by towering cliffs. The setting sun cast long shadows across the ground, and the air was filled with the scent of pine and earth.

Kaelen leaned against a nearby boulder, his breath coming in ragged gasps. Alyssa dropped to one knee beside him, her own exhaustion evident in the way her shoulders sagged.

"We're not far ahead of them," Alyssa said between breaths. "We need to be careful. They won't stop until they find us."

Kaelen nodded, his mind racing as he tried to assess their situation. "We need to keep moving, but we also need to rest— just for a moment. We can't afford to be caught off guard."

Alyssa agreed, and they both took a few moments to catch their breath, the silence of the clearing providing a brief respite from the tension that had been building since their escape from the Nexus Shrine.

Even as they rested, Kaelen couldn't shake the feeling that something was wrong—something beyond the threat of the Legion of Shadows. There was a new presence, one that had been lurking at the edges of his awareness since they had left the shrine. It was subtle, almost imperceptible, but it was there—a shadow that followed them, watching, waiting.

Kaelen looked at Alyssa, his expression serious. "Do you feel it? There's someone else out there—someone different from the Legion."

Alyssa's eyes narrowed, her hand instinctively going to her weapon. "I've felt it too. It's like we're being hunted."

Kaelen's grip tightened on the gauntlet. "The Shadow Keeper must have sent someone—someone skilled, someone who can track us."

Alyssa's gaze swept the clearing, her senses on high alert. "We need to move. We can't let them catch us."

Kaelen nodded, pushing himself away from the boulder. "Let's go. We'll figure out our next move as we go."

They set off again, moving quickly through the forest as the shadows lengthened around them. The feeling of being watched, of being pursued, grew stronger with each step, and Kaelen knew they were running out of time. The forest was dense and unforgiving, the terrain rugged and treacherous, but they pressed on, driven by the knowledge that stopping would mean certain capture—or worse.

As they made their way through a particularly thick patch of trees, Kaelen suddenly felt a shift in the air—a change in the flow of time, subtle but unmistakable. He stopped in his tracks, his senses on high alert, and held up a hand to signal Alyssa to do the same.

"What is it?" Alyssa whispered, her voice tense.

Kaelen's eyes scanned the forest around them, his heart pounding in his chest. "I'm not sure... but something's here. Something's close."

Before Alyssa could respond, a figure emerged from the shadows, moving with a speed and silence that was almost inhuman. The figure was tall and lean, clad in dark, form-fitting armor that seemed to blend seamlessly with the surrounding forest. Their face was hidden behind a mask that glowed with an eerie, green light, and they moved with the grace and precision of a predator.

Kaelen's blood ran cold as he realized who—what—they were facing. "The Time Hunter."

The Time Hunter was a figure of legend among those who knew the secrets of time travel—a skilled tracker and assassin, trained to hunt down and eliminate anyone who posed a threat to the stability of the timeline. They were relentless, efficient, and utterly devoid of mercy.

The Time Hunter's voice was low and cold, each word measured and precise. "Kaelen Mercer. You've been marked for elimination."

Kaelen's grip tightened on the gauntlet, his mind racing as he tried to figure out their next move. They were outmatched, outpaced, and there was no way they could fight the Time Hunter head-on. Their only chance was to outthink their pursuer—to use the gauntlet's power to create an opportunity to escape.

Without another word, Kaelen turned and bolted into the forest, Alyssa right behind him. The Time Hunter didn't hesitate, moving with a speed and agility that made it clear this would be no ordinary chase.

As they ran, Kaelen focused on the gauntlet, reaching out to the flow of time around them. He could feel the power of the gauntlet responding to his intent, the energy crackling around him as he began to manipulate the temporal field. He needed to create a distortion—something that would throw the Time Hunter off their trail, even if only for a moment.

"Kaelen, what are you doing?" Alyssa's voice was breathless with both exertion and concern.

"Buying us time," Kaelen replied, his voice strained as he concentrated on the gauntlet.

The forest around them began to blur as Kaelen slowed the flow of time, creating a temporal distortion that stretched the seconds into minutes. The world around them seemed to move in slow motion, the sounds of the forest fading into a low hum as the temporal field took hold.

The Time Hunter was relentless, unaffected by the distortion, moving through the altered time as if it were nothing more than an inconvenience. Kaelen's heart pounded in his chest as he realized the Time Hunter's mastery of time was far beyond anything he had encountered before.

"We need to keep moving!" Alyssa urged, her eyes wide with fear.

Kaelen pushed himself harder, the strain of maintaining the temporal distortion weighing heavily on him. He knew it wouldn't be enough—not against an enemy like this. They needed something more, something that would give them a real chance to escape.

As they rounded a bend in the forest, Kaelen spotted a narrow ravine up ahead, the rocky terrain offering a potential advantage. He didn't hesitate, leading Alyssa toward the ravine with the Time Hunter still hot on their heels.

"We can use the terrain to our advantage," Kaelen said, his voice tight with determination. "Follow my lead."

They reached the edge of the ravine and began to climb down the steep slope, the loose rocks making every step treacherous. The Time Hunter was right behind them, moving with the same unnerving precision, but the difficult terrain slowed their pursuit, giving Kaelen and Alyssa a brief window of opportunity.

Kaelen focused on the gauntlet once more, this time creating a temporal decoy—a shadowy, distorted version of himself that would lead the Time Hunter in the wrong direction. The decoy split off from them, running down a side path as the real Kaelen and Alyssa continued their descent into the ravine.

The trick worked, if only for a moment. The Time Hunter hesitated, assessing the decoy, before realizing the ruse and continuing the pursuit. In that brief moment of confusion was enough to give Kaelen and Alyssa a small head start.

They reached the bottom of the ravine, the steep walls towering above them, and continued running along the narrow path that wound through the rocky terrain. The sounds of the forest above were muffled, the air growing cooler as they moved deeper into the ravine.

Kaelen knew they couldn't keep this up forever. The Time Hunter was too skilled, too relentless, and they were running out of options. They couldn't stop—not when they were so close to finding the Nexus Crystal.

As they rounded another bend, Kaelen spotted a narrow cave entrance hidden among the rocks. It was a risky move, but it might be their best chance to hide and regroup.

"In here!" Kaelen called to Alyssa, pointing to the cave.

They ducked into the cave, the darkness swallowing them as they moved deeper inside. The walls were cold and damp, the air thick with the scent of earth and stone. They moved quickly, the narrow passage forcing them to crouch as they made their way deeper into the cave.

Kaelen could feel the Time Hunter's presence growing stronger, the pressure of the pursuit weighing heavily on him. As they reached the end of the passage, he spotted a small alcove—a hidden niche that could offer them a brief moment of safety.

They squeezed into the alcove, the darkness enveloping them as they pressed themselves against the cold stone walls. Kaelen could feel Alyssa's breath, quick and shallow, beside him, and he knew they were both on the brink of exhaustion.

"We can't stay here long," Alyssa whispered, her voice trembling with both fear and adrenaline.

Kaelen nodded, his mind racing as he tried to come up with a plan. "We just need to catch our breath—then we'll move."

The silence in the cave was oppressive, the sound of their breathing loud in the confined space. Kaelen's heart pounded in his chest, the gauntlet's power pulsing faintly against his arm as he tried to calm his racing thoughts.

After a few moments, Alyssa spoke again, her voice soft but filled with determination. "We're going to make it, Kaelen. We have to."

Kaelen looked at her, the resolve in her eyes giving him strength. "We will. We're too close to stop now."

They waited a few more moments, the darkness of the cave providing them with a brief respite from the relentless pursuit. Kaelen knew they couldn't stay hidden forever—the Time Hunter was too skilled, too experienced to be thrown off their trail for long.

"We need to keep moving," Kaelen finally said, his voice firm. "If we stay here, we'll be trapped."

Alyssa nodded, her expression steely. "Lead the way."

They cautiously emerged from the alcove, their senses on high alert as they moved back through the narrow passage. The air was thick with tension, every sound amplified by the silence of the cave.

As they reached the entrance of the cave, Kaelen paused, listening carefully for any sign of the Time Hunter. The forest outside was eerily quiet, the setting sun casting long shadows across the ground.

"We're clear for now," Kaelen said, though his voice was tinged with uncertainty. "We need to move fast."

They left the cave and continued their journey through the forest, their pace quick but cautious. The encounter with the Time

Hunter had shaken them both, but it had also strengthened their resolve. They knew now that they were being hunted—relentlessly, methodically—but they couldn't let that stop them.

As they moved through the forest, Kaelen and Alyssa took brief moments to study the clues they had gathered from the Nexus Shrine. The inscriptions, the symbols, the fragmented pieces of information—all of it pointed to a specific moment in time where the Nexus Crystal might be hidden.

The clues were cryptic, fragmented, requiring them to piece together a coherent picture from the information they had. Kaelen focused on the gauntlet, using its power to help him interpret the temporal hints, but it was slow going. Each piece of the puzzle only seemed to raise more questions, but they were getting closer.

"This symbol," Alyssa said, pointing to a particular inscription they had found in the shrine. "It's the same as the one on the gauntlet. It must be connected to the location of the crystal."

Kaelen studied the symbol, his mind racing as he tried to make the connection. "It's a marker—a signpost in time. If we can figure out what it means, we can trace the crystal's path."

They continued to work through the clues, their movements careful and deliberate as they deciphered the information. The gauntlet's power pulsed with a steady rhythm, resonating with the energy of the Nexus as Kaelen focused on the task at hand.

Even as they worked, the threat of the Time Hunter loomed over them, a constant reminder of the danger they were in. Kaelen could feel the pressure mounting, the weight of their mission growing heavier with each passing moment.

Then, just as they were beginning to make progress, Kaelen felt it—a sudden, sharp spike in the temporal field. It was a warning, a signal that the Time Hunter was close, too close.

"We need to go," Kaelen said urgently, his heart pounding. "Now."

They abandoned their work and set off again, moving quickly through the forest as the shadows lengthened around them. The Time Hunter was relentless, a shadow that followed them, always just out of sight but never far behind.

As they reached the edge of the forest, Kaelen spotted a narrow pass between two cliffs—a potential escape route that could buy them some time. It was risky, the pass narrow and treacherous, with little room for error.

"We can use the pass to slow them down," Kaelen said, his voice tight with determination. "But we need to move fast."

Alyssa nodded, and they made their way toward the pass, the rocky terrain making every step a challenge. The sun was setting, the light fading quickly as they navigated the narrow path between the cliffs.

As they reached the midpoint of the pass, Kaelen suddenly felt a sharp, searing pain in his head—a familiar sensation that signaled a temporal disturbance. He staggered, clutching his temple as the world around him seemed to blur and distort.

"Kaelen!" Alyssa's voice was filled with concern as she reached out to steady him. "What's happening?"

Kaelen shook his head, trying to clear the fog from his mind. "It's the Time Hunter—they're manipulating the temporal field."

The pain intensified, the distortion growing stronger as the Time Hunter closed in on them. Kaelen's vision swam, the gauntlet's power flaring wildly as he struggled to maintain control.

"We need to get out of here," Kaelen said through gritted teeth, the strain evident in his voice. "They're trying to trap us."

Alyssa helped him to his feet, her expression filled with determination. "We're not stopping now. Come on—we'll make it."

They pushed forward, the pass narrowing around them as the temporal distortion threatened to overwhelm them. The Time Hunter was closing in, their presence a dark, oppressive force that seemed to twist the very fabric of reality.

Kaelen refused to give in. He focused on the gauntlet, drawing on its power to create a temporal barrier—a shield that would protect them from the worst of the distortion. The gauntlet responded, the energy crackling around them as the barrier took shape.

The distortion lessened, the pressure easing as the temporal field stabilized. The Time Hunter was still close, their relentless pursuit driving Kaelen and Alyssa to keep moving, to push through the pain and exhaustion.

Finally, after what felt like an eternity, they emerged from the pass, the rocky terrain giving way to a wide, open plain. The sun had set, the sky now a deep, inky black, the stars twinkling faintly overhead.

Kaelen and Alyssa didn't stop, didn't even look back as they crossed the plain, the open space giving them a brief respite from the Time Hunter's relentless pursuit. They knew it wouldn't last—the Time Hunter was too skilled, too determined to let them go so easily.

As they reached the far side of the plain, Kaelen finally allowed himself to slow down, his breath coming in ragged gasps as he tried to regain his strength. Alyssa was beside him, her face pale but resolute.

"We made it," she said, her voice barely above a whisper.

Kaelen nodded, though the weight of their mission still pressed heavily on his mind. "But we're not safe—not yet."

They took a brief moment to catch their breath, the silence of the night a stark contrast to the chaos they had just escaped. The Time Hunter was still out there, still hunting them, but for now, they had bought themselves a little time.

"We need to figure out where the crystal is hidden," Kaelen said, his voice firm. "We're getting closer—I can feel it. We need to move quickly before the Time Hunter catches up."

Alyssa nodded, her expression serious. "Let's go. We can't afford to waste any more time."

They set off again, their pace quick but cautious as they made their way across the plain. The stars overhead provided a faint light to guide their way, but the darkness was still thick, the shadows deep and foreboding.

As they walked, Kaelen and Alyssa continued to work through the clues they had gathered, their minds racing as they pieced together the information. The symbols, the inscriptions, the fragmented hints—they all pointed to a specific moment in time, a place where the Nexus Crystal might have been hidden.

"It's like a puzzle," Alyssa said, her voice thoughtful. "Each piece is connected, but we need to figure out how they all fit together."

Kaelen nodded, the gauntlet's power pulsing faintly as he concentrated. "The crystal was hidden in a moment in time, a place where it would be safe from those who would misuse it. If we can find that moment, we can find the crystal."

They worked through the night, their movements careful and deliberate as they deciphered the clues. The gauntlet's power guided them, helping them interpret the temporal hints and piece together the puzzle.

And finally, just as the first light of dawn began to break over the horizon, they had it—the next lead, the next piece of the puzzle that would bring them closer to the Nexus Crystal.

"This is it," Kaelen said, his voice filled with both relief and determination. "We've found the next step."

Alyssa looked at him, her eyes bright with hope. "Then let's go. We're not stopping now."

They set off toward their new destination, the rising sun casting long shadows across the plain as they moved forward. The Time Hunter was still out there, still hunting them, but Kaelen and Alyssa were determined to stay one step ahead.

The journey was far from over, but they were closer now closer to finding the Nexus Crystal, closer to stopping the Shadow Keeper, closer to protecting the future.

And no matter what challenges lay ahead, they would face them together.

Chapter 11

The world shimmered and shifted around Kaelen as he and Alyssa emerged from the temporal passage, the energy of the gauntlet still humming faintly against his arm. The transition between times was always disorienting, but this time it was particularly unsettling. The air around them was heavy, thick with the scent of earth and the sound of distant, rhythmic drums. They had arrived.

The landscape was unlike anything Kaelen had ever seen. Towering trees with thick, gnarled roots surrounded them, their canopies stretching high into the sky, blotting out much of the sunlight. The ground was soft and damp beneath their feet, covered in a dense layer of moss and fallen leaves. In the distance, the outline of what looked like an ancient structure rose from the forest floor, partially obscured by the undergrowth.

Kaelen took a deep breath, trying to steady himself after the jarring experience of time travel. "This must be it," he said, his voice hushed as he took in their surroundings. "The time and place the clues pointed to."

Alyssa nodded, her eyes scanning the dense forest around them. "We need to be careful. We don't know what we're walking into."

Kaelen agreed, his hand instinctively going to the gauntlet. The energy of the Nexus Crystal had guided them here, but the sense of unease that had settled over him since their arrival was impossible to ignore. Something about this place felt... off, as if the very air was charged with the remnants of ancient power.

They began to move cautiously through the forest, the thick undergrowth making every step a challenge. The rhythmic sound of drums grew louder as they approached the ancient structure, its silhouette becoming clearer through the trees. It was a temple of some kind, its stone walls covered in intricate carvings and symbols that seemed to pulse with a faint, otherworldly light.

"This place is ancient," Alyssa whispered as they neared the entrance to the temple. "Older than anything we've encountered before."

Kaelen nodded; his gaze fixed on the carvings that adorned the temple's entrance. The symbols were familiar, similar to those they had seen in the Nexus Shrine, but they were older, more primitive, as if they were the original version of the symbols that had been passed down through the ages.

"This must be where the Nexus Crystal was hidden," Kaelen said, his voice filled with both awe and trepidation. "Or at least where it was once kept."

They entered the temple, the air inside cool and still, the faint echo of their footsteps the only sound in the cavernous space. The walls were covered in more carvings, depicting scenes of rituals and figures shrouded in shadow, their faces obscured by time and the elements. The energy of the Nexus was stronger here, pulsing faintly through the stone walls, as if the crystal's power had seeped into the very fabric of the temple.

As they moved deeper into the temple, Kaelen began to feel a strange sensation in the back of his mind, a faint whisper that seemed to call out to him from the shadows. It was subtle at first, like a distant memory just out of reach, but it grew stronger the further they went.

"Do you hear that?" Kaelen asked, his voice barely above a whisper.

Alyssa frowned, looking around. "Hear what?"

Kaelen hesitated, unsure how to explain what he was experiencing. "It's like a… whisper, but not with words. It's coming from the walls, from the stone itself."

Alyssa's expression turned serious, and she moved closer to him, her hand resting on her weapon. "We need to be careful. This place might be more than just a temple—it could be a trap."

Kaelen nodded, but the whispering continued to grow stronger, tugging at the edges of his consciousness. It was as if the temple was trying to communicate with him, to show him something important. He placed a hand on the wall, the cold stone rough under his fingertips, and closed his eyes, focusing on the sensation.

The moment he made contact, the world around him seemed to dissolve, the stone walls fading into darkness. Kaelen felt himself being pulled into a vision, the whispering voices growing louder, more insistent, until they became a deafening roar.

When the darkness cleared, Kaelen found himself standing in a vast, open space, the sky above him a deep, swirling mass of storm clouds. The ground beneath his feet was barren and cracked, stretching out in all directions as far as the eye could see. The air was thick with the scent of smoke and ash, the distant rumble of thunder echoing across the desolate landscape.

In the distance, Kaelen could see a group of figures gathered around a large, glowing object that pulsed with a brilliant, golden light. The figures were cloaked in shadows, their faces obscured, but Kaelen could feel the power radiating from them, a raw, untamed energy that resonated with the gauntlet on his arm.

"This is it," a voice said, low and commanding. "The source of all time, the key to the future."

Kaelen recognized the voice—it was the Shadow Keeper. He watched as the cloaked figure stepped forward; his hand

172

outstretched toward the glowing object. The energy of the Nexus Crystal flared in response, its light intensifying as it pulsed with the power of the timeline itself.

"This power will be mine," the Shadow Keeper continued, his voice filled with both awe and determination. "With it, I will reshape reality, bend time to my will, and create a world where I alone hold the key to the future."

Kaelen felt a surge of anger and fear as he realized what he was witnessing—a moment from the past, a glimpse into the Shadow Keeper's origins. The vision was both a warning and a reminder of the stakes they were facing. The Nexus Crystal was the keystone of the timeline, the source of its stability, and the Shadow Keeper was determined to claim it for himself.

The vision shifted again, the barren landscape fading into a different scene—this time, a grand hall filled with light and warmth. The walls were lined with ornate tapestries and golden statues, and at the center of the hall stood a massive throne, upon which sat a figure shrouded in shadow.

Kaelen watched as the Shadow Keeper approached the throne, his expression one of reverence and determination. The figure on the throne raised a hand, and the room was filled with a blinding light, the energy of the Nexus Crystal resonating with the power of the gauntlet.

"You have done well," the figure on the throne said, their voice deep and commanding. "But the power of the Nexus is not yours to claim. It belongs to the timeline, to the Time Keepers. You must understand this, or you will bring about the end of all things."

The Shadow Keeper hesitated, his hand hovering over the gauntlet on his arm. "I seek only to protect the timeline, to ensure its stability."

The figure on the throne shook their head, their voice filled with both sadness and resolve. "Power cannot protect—it can only corrupt. The Nexus Crystal is not a weapon, but a tool to preserve the flow of time. If you continue down this path, you will destroy everything you seek to protect."

The vision blurred again, the light fading into darkness as Kaelen felt himself being pulled back to the present. He staggered, his hand slipping from the wall as the vision released its grip on him.

"Kaelen!" Alyssa's voice was filled with concern as she caught him before he could fall. "What happened? Are you alright?"

Kaelen took a deep breath, his heart pounding as he tried to make sense of what he had seen. "I... I saw the past. The Shadow Keeper, the Nexus Crystal—it all started here."

Alyssa's eyes widened, her expression filled with both shock and understanding. "What did you see?"

Kaelen explained the vision as best he could, describing the Shadow Keeper's attempt to claim the Nexus Crystal and the warning he had received from the figure on the throne. As he spoke, he realized the gravity of what he had witnessed—the Nexus Crystal was more than just a powerful artifact; it was the key to the stability of the entire timeline.

"The Shadow Keeper was warned," Kaelen said, his voice low and filled with dread. "He was told that the Nexus Crystal wasn't his to claim, that it was meant to preserve time, not control it. But he didn't listen. He's determined to reshape reality, no matter the cost."

Alyssa's expression hardened, her resolve clear. "Then we have to stop him. We can't let him get his hands on the crystal."

Kaelen nodded, though the weight of the task before them seemed even heavier now. They had to find the Nexus Crystal, to protect it from the Shadow Keeper and ensure that the timeline remained intact. The visions had also raised new questions— questions about Kaelen's own role in this, about his connection to the gauntlet and the Nexus Crystal.

Before they could delve further into their thoughts, a familiar and chilling presence made itself known. Kaelen and Alyssa tensed as they felt the unmistakable energy of the Time Hunter approaching. The realization sent a jolt of fear through them—there was no more time to dwell on visions or revelations. They had to act.

"Let's move," Kaelen said urgently, his senses on high alert. "The Time Hunter is close."

They turned to leave the temple, but as they moved toward the entrance, the air around them seemed to thicken, the shadows growing deeper and more oppressive. Kaelen could feel the temporal energy shifting, warping the space around them, a sure sign that the Time Hunter was manipulating the timeline to trap them.

"We're not going to make it out this way," Alyssa said, her voice filled with urgency. "We need to find another exit."

Kaelen scanned the temple, his mind racing as he searched for a way out. The Time Hunter was close, too close, and the walls of the temple seemed to close in around them, the shadows growing darker and more menacing.

"There!" Kaelen pointed to a narrow passage hidden behind one of the large stone carvings. "That might be our only chance."

They dashed toward the passage, the sound of the Time Hunter's approach echoing through the temple. The passage was narrow and winding, the walls pressing in on them as they moved deeper into the darkness. The air grew colder, the faint light from the entrance fading as they descended further into the temple's depths.

Kaelen could feel the gauntlet's power reacting to the temporal distortion, the energy crackling around him as he tried to maintain control. The Time Hunter was relentless, manipulating the flow of time to catch them, but Kaelen knew they couldn't give in.

"We have to keep moving," Kaelen said, his voice strained. "If we stop now, we're done."

They continued down the passage, the path becoming steeper and more treacherous. The sound of the Time Hunter's footsteps grew louder, closer, as the walls of the passage began to warp and shift, the temporal distortion making it difficult to distinguish reality from illusion.

Alyssa grabbed Kaelen's arm, pulling him back as the passageway suddenly dropped off into a deep chasm. "Watch out!"

Kaelen skidded to a halt just in time, his heart racing as he peered over the edge of the chasm. The drop was steep, the bottom shrouded in darkness, but there was no turning back now. The Time Hunter was closing in, and they had no other option.

"We have to jump," Kaelen said, his voice steady despite the fear gnawing at him. "It's the only way."

Alyssa hesitated for a split second, her eyes locking with Kaelen's. Then she nodded, her expression resolute. "Together."

They took a deep breath, bracing themselves for the leap. Kaelen focused on the gauntlet, using its power to slow the flow of time around them, giving them a better chance of surviving the jump. Then, without another word, they jumped.

The world seemed to slow to a crawl as they fell, the wind rushing past them as the chasm yawned below. Kaelen held tightly to Alyssa's hand, the gauntlet's power creating a protective barrier around them as they plummeted into the darkness.

Time itself seemed to blur, the boundaries between moments dissolving as they fell deeper into the chasm. Kaelen's mind raced, the visions from earlier still fresh in his memory, but he forced himself to focus on the present—on surviving.

With a jarring impact, they hit the bottom of the chasm, the protective barrier absorbing much of the force but still leaving them shaken and bruised. Kaelen groaned as he pulled himself to his feet, his body aching from the fall. Alyssa was beside him, her breathing labored but steady.

"We made it," she said, her voice filled with both relief and disbelief.

Kaelen nodded, though the danger was far from over. They were in the depths of the temple now, far below the surface, and the Time Hunter was still somewhere above them, hunting them with relentless determination.

"We need to keep moving," Kaelen said, his voice firm despite the exhaustion that weighed heavily on him. "We can't let the Time Hunter catch up."

Alyssa nodded, and together they began to move through the darkness, the faint light of the gauntlet guiding their way. The chasm led to a network of tunnels, winding and twisting through the bowels of the temple, and Kaelen could feel the ancient power that still resonated within these walls.

As they navigated the tunnels, Kaelen's thoughts turned to the visions he had seen—the Shadow Keeper's origins, the warning he had received, and the looming threat of the Nexus Crystal falling into the wrong hands. The weight of their mission seemed even greater now, but so too did Kaelen's determination to see it through.

"We're getting closer," Kaelen said, his voice filled with a quiet resolve. "The clues we've gathered—they all point to this place, this time. We're on the right path."

Alyssa looked at him, her expression serious. "But the Time Hunter won't stop. We need to stay ahead of them, no matter what."

Kaelen knew she was right. The Time Hunter was relentless, and the challenges they faced would only grow more difficult. But they had come too far to turn back now.

Finally, after what felt like hours of navigating the dark tunnels, they emerged into a large, open chamber. The walls were lined with ancient carvings, similar to those they had seen in the upper levels of the temple, but these were different—more detailed, more intricate, as if they held the final pieces of the puzzle they had been searching for.

Kaelen approached the carvings, his eyes scanning the symbols and inscriptions with a sense of urgency. The gauntlet pulsed with energy, resonating with the power that still lingered in this place, and Kaelen could feel the answers they sought just out of reach.

"We're close," Kaelen said, his voice filled with both hope and determination. "I can feel it."

Before they could decipher the final clues, the air around them seemed to shift, the shadows deepening as a familiar presence made itself known. The Time Hunter had found them.

Kaelen and Alyssa tensed, their senses on high alert as the temperature in the chamber dropped, the oppressive weight of the Time Hunter's power pressing down on them. They had no more room to run—this would be their final confrontation.

The Time Hunter emerged from the shadows, their figure cloaked in darkness, the eerie green glow of their mask casting an unnatural light across the chamber. Their voice was cold and unyielding, each word a dagger in the still air.

"You cannot escape time, Kaelen Mercer. It is both your master and your prison."

Kaelen's heart pounded in his chest, but he refused to back down. He knew the Time Hunter was powerful, skilled beyond anything they had encountered before, but he also knew that they couldn't afford to lose this battle—not when they were so close.

"We make our own fate," Kaelen said, his voice steady despite the fear that gnawed at him. "And we're not giving up."

The Time Hunter's gaze shifted to Alyssa, their voice dripping with contempt. "You are out of your depth. The Nexus Crystal will be mine, and you will be nothing but a forgotten whisper in the annals of time."

The tension in the chamber was thick, the air charged with the energy of the impending confrontation. Kaelen could feel the power of the gauntlet surging within him, responding to the threat before them. This was it—the moment where everything would be decided.

"Kaelen, we have to do this," Alyssa said, her voice filled with both determination and resolve. "Together."

Kaelen nodded; his gaze locked on the Time Hunter. "Together."

With a burst of energy, the Time Hunter lunged forward, their movements fluid and precise, like a shadow striking in the dead of night. Kaelen reacted instantly, using the gauntlet to create a temporal shield, deflecting the Time Hunter's attack with a surge of power.

The chamber erupted into chaos, the walls echoing with the sounds of their battle. Kaelen and Alyssa fought with everything they had, their movements perfectly in sync as they used the environment to their advantage, weaving through the ancient carvings and using the gauntlet's power to create temporal distortions that threw the Time Hunter off balance.

The Time Hunter was relentless, their attacks growing more ferocious with each passing moment. Kaelen could feel the strain of the gauntlet's power, the energy within it fluctuating as he pushed it to its limits. He knew they couldn't keep this up forever—something had to give.

As the battle reached its climax, Kaelen felt a sudden surge of power from the gauntlet, a final burst of energy that flooded his senses. The carvings on the walls seemed to come to life, the ancient symbols glowing with a brilliant light as the power of the Nexus Crystal resonated through the chamber.

Kaelen focused all his energy, channeling the power of the gauntlet into a single, decisive attack. The air crackled with energy as the gauntlet unleashed a wave of temporal force, a shockwave that tore through the chamber and slammed into the Time Hunter with devastating force.

The Time Hunter staggered, their form flickering as the temporal energy disrupted their connection to the timeline. For a moment, it seemed as though they might regain their footing, but then the flickering intensified, and with a final, echoing cry, the Time Hunter vanished, dissipating into the ether.

The chamber fell silent, the oppressive weight of the Time Hunter's presence lifting as the energy in the air began to dissipate. Kaelen and Alyssa stood still for a moment, their breaths coming in ragged gasps as they processed what had just happened.

"We did it," Alyssa said, her voice filled with both relief and disbelief.

Kaelen nodded, though the weight of their victory was tempered by the knowledge that their journey was far from over. They had survived the Time Hunter's attack, but the true challenge still lay ahead finding the Nexus Crystal and stopping the Shadow Keeper once and for all.

"We need to keep going," Kaelen said, his voice steady despite the exhaustion that weighed heavily on him. "The Nexus Crystal is still out there, and we're closer than ever."

Alyssa looked at him, her expression serious but filled with determination. "Then let's finish this."

They turned to the ancient carvings on the walls, the final pieces of the puzzle still waiting to be deciphered. The gauntlet pulsed with energy, guiding Kaelen as he studied the symbols, piecing together the clues that would lead them to the Nexus Crystal.

As they worked, Kaelen couldn't shake the feeling that they were being watched—that the shadows in the chamber held secrets yet to be revealed. He pushed the thought aside, focusing on the task at hand.

The visions, the battles, the challenges they had faced—it had all led to this moment. They were on the brink of discovering the truth, of uncovering the location of the Nexus Crystal, and nothing would stop them now.

Kaelen and Alyssa worked tirelessly; their resolve unshakable as they deciphered the final clues. The light from the gauntlet illuminated the ancient symbols, revealing the path they had been searching for all along.

"We've got it," Kaelen said, his voice filled with both relief and anticipation. "The Nexus Crystal—it's hidden in a moment in time, a place where it will be safe from those who seek to misuse its power."

Alyssa nodded, her eyes bright with hope. "Then we know where to go."

They turned to leave the chamber, their mission clear, their path set. The journey ahead would be difficult, the dangers they faced even greater, but they were ready.

Together, they would find the Nexus Crystal, stop the Shadow Keeper, and protect the timeline from those who sought to control it.

The shadows of the past might still linger, but Kaelen and Alyssa were focused on the future—on the destiny they were determined to shape.

And no matter what challenges lay ahead, they would face them together.

Chapter 12

The ancient symbols carved into the walls of the chamber pulsed faintly with light as Kaelen and Alyssa worked side by side, piecing together the final clues that would lead them to the Nexus Crystal. The air was thick with anticipation, every whisper of wind through the stone corridors carrying with it a sense of urgency. They had come so far, and the end was almost in sight, but the challenges they faced seemed to grow with each passing moment.

Kaelen wiped a bead of sweat from his brow, his mind racing as he examined the intricate carvings. The symbols were a complex puzzle, each one connected to the next in a web of meanings and references that stretched across time itself. The gauntlet on his arm hummed softly, resonating with the energy in the chamber, guiding his thoughts as he tried to make sense of the ancient language.

"This is it," Kaelen said, his voice barely above a whisper as he traced a line of symbols with his finger. "The final clue. It's pointing to a specific location, a point in time where the Nexus Crystal was hidden."

Alyssa leaned in closer, her eyes scanning the symbols with a sharp, analytical gaze. "The symbols are coordinates, but they're encoded. We'll need to decode them to find the exact time and place."

Kaelen nodded, his mind already working through the possibilities. The process was slow and meticulous, each symbol holding layers of meaning that needed to be unraveled before they could understand the full message. They were making progress, and with each new discovery, the path to the Nexus Crystal became clearer.

As they worked, Kaelen began to notice a change in the air around them. It was subtle at first, a faint shift in the temperature, a slight distortion in the light that filtered through the chamber. As the minutes passed, the feeling grew stronger, more oppressive, until it was impossible to ignore.

Kaelen paused, his hand hovering over the symbols as he looked around the chamber. "Do you feel that?"

Alyssa nodded, her expression tense. "It's the Shadow Keeper's influence. It's growing stronger."

Kaelen's grip tightened on the gauntlet, the device pulsing with a faint, rhythmic energy that echoed the dark power that seemed to seep into the chamber. The Shadow Keeper was growing more powerful, his reach extending across time and space as he drew closer to his goal. And as his power grew, so too did the threat to the timeline.

"We need to move faster," Kaelen said, his voice laced with urgency. "The longer we stay here, the more dangerous it becomes."

They redoubled their efforts, their hands moving quickly over the symbols as they decoded the final message. Even as they worked, the Shadow Keeper's presence continued to grow, the air around them thickening with the weight of his influence. Kaelen could feel it pressing down on him, a dark force that threatened to pull him under, to consume him in the same way it had consumed so many before him.

He couldn't afford to give in. Not now. Not when they were so close.

Finally, after what felt like hours of intense focus, they deciphered the final symbols, revealing the location and time where the Nexus Crystal had been hidden.

"It's a temple," Alyssa said, her voice filled with a mixture of awe and relief. "An ancient temple hidden deep in the mountains, far from any civilization. The crystal was hidden there centuries ago, protected by powerful wards and temporal barriers."

Kaelen's heart raced as he processed the information. "That's where we need to go. Getting there won't be easy. The Shadow Keeper knows we're close, and he'll do everything he can to stop us."

Alyssa nodded, her expression resolute. "Then we'll have to be ready for anything. We've come too far to turn back now."

With the final puzzle solved, they began to prepare for the journey ahead. The temple was located in a remote and treacherous region, a place where time itself was unstable, and the influence of the Nexus Crystal had warped the very fabric of reality. Reaching it would require all of their skill, courage, and the full power of the gauntlet.

They gathered what supplies they could, making sure they were prepared for the dangers that lay ahead. Kaelen took a moment to adjust the gauntlet, feeling the energy coursing through it as he synchronized it with the coordinates they had uncovered. The device was more than just a tool now—it was a part of him, a connection to the power that would guide them to the Nexus Crystal.

As they packed their belongings and prepared to leave the chamber, Kaelen took a moment to look at Alyssa. She was focused, determined, but there was a softness in her eyes that spoke of the bond they had forged over the course of their journey. They had faced so much together, and now, as they stood on the brink of their greatest challenge, Kaelen felt a deep sense of gratitude for her presence.

"Alyssa," Kaelen said, his voice soft but filled with emotion. "I couldn't have done any of this without you. Whatever happens next, I want you to know how much you mean to me."

Alyssa turned to him, her eyes meeting his with a look of warmth and understanding. "Kaelen, we're in this together. I'm not going anywhere. We'll see this through—together."

They shared a brief, but meaningful moment of connection before turning their attention back to the task at hand. The temple awaited, and with it, the final confrontation with the Shadow Keeper.

Just as they were about to set off, the air in the chamber shifted once more, the temperature plummeting as a sudden wave of dark energy washed over them. Kaelen and Alyssa tensed, their senses on high alert as they realized what was happening.

"We're not alone," Kaelen said, his voice tense as he scanned the chamber.

Before they could react, the entrance to the chamber exploded in a burst of dark energy, the force of the blast sending them both tumbling to the ground. Kaelen scrambled to his feet, his heart pounding as he saw the figures emerging from the smoke and debris.

A group of Shadow Keepers' minions, clad in dark armor and wielding weapons wreathed in shadow, advanced toward them, their eyes glowing with a malevolent light. At the head of the group was a figure Kaelen recognized all too well—the Shadow Keeper's lieutenant, the same one they had encountered before.

"This ends here, Kaelen Mercer," the lieutenant said, his voice echoing with the power of the Shadow Keeper. "You've come far, but your journey is over."

Kaelen's grip tightened on the gauntlet, the device responding with a surge of energy as he prepared for the battle ahead. "We're not giving up," Kaelen said, his voice steady despite the fear that gnawed at him. "Not when we're so close."

The chamber erupted into chaos as the Shadow Keeper's forces attacked, their dark energy filling the air with an oppressive weight that threatened to crush Kaelen and Alyssa under its force. Kaelen moved quickly, using the gauntlet to deflect their attacks, creating temporal distortions that slowed their movements and gave him the advantage.

The Shadow Keeper's lieutenant was relentless, his attacks precise and deadly as he pressed forward, determined to end their mission once and for all. Kaelen could feel the strain of the gauntlet's power as he pushed it to its limits, the energy within it fluctuating wildly as he fought to maintain control.

Alyssa was by his side, her movements fluid and graceful as she fought off their attackers, her weapon flashing in the dim

light of the chamber. They were outnumbered, and the relentless assault was taking its toll.

"We can't keep this up!" Alyssa shouted over the din of battle, her voice filled with both determination and desperation. "We need to get out of here!"

Kaelen knew she was right, but escaping wouldn't be easy. The Shadow Keeper's forces were closing in, their attacks growing more ferocious with each passing moment. They needed a plan, and they needed it fast.

With a burst of inspiration, Kaelen focused on the gauntlet, channeling its power into a single, focused point. The device responded with a surge of energy, the symbols etched into its surface glowing brightly as he unleashed a wave of temporal force that slammed into their attackers, sending them reeling back.

"Now!" Kaelen shouted, grabbing Alyssa's hand as they bolted for the exit.

They raced through the corridors of the temple, the sounds of battle fading behind them as they put as much distance as possible between themselves and the Shadow Keeper's forces. The temple seemed to twist and shift around them, the unstable temporal energy creating a labyrinth of passages that made it difficult to find their way.

Kaelen's mind was sharp, his senses heightened by the adrenaline that coursed through his veins. He guided them through the twisting corridors, his grip on Alyssa's hand never faltering as they moved closer to the exit.

Finally, after what felt like an eternity, they burst through the temple's outer gates, the cool night air hitting their faces as they emerged into the open. The landscape was bathed in the soft glow of the moon, the distant mountains casting long shadows across the ground.

They didn't stop running until they were sure they were far enough from the temple to be safe. Only then did Kaelen allow himself to slow down, his breath coming in ragged gasps as he collapsed against a large boulder.

Alyssa was beside him, her chest heaving as she tried to catch her breath. "That was too close," she said, her voice filled with both relief and exhaustion.

Kaelen nodded, though his mind was still racing with the events that had just transpired. They had barely escaped with their lives, and the Shadow Keeper's forces were more determined than ever to stop them. They had the coordinates, the final piece of the puzzle that would lead them to the Nexus Crystal.

"We need to keep moving," Kaelen said, though his voice was laced with weariness. "The Shadow Keeper won't stop until he has the crystal, and neither can we."

Alyssa agreed, though the weight of their mission was clearly taking its toll on both of them. They had faced so many challenges, so many battles, and the end was finally in sight. The path ahead would be the most difficult yet.

As they began to gather their strength for the journey ahead, Kaelen couldn't shake the feeling that something was still amiss. The Shadow Keeper's influence had grown stronger, his power more insidious, and Kaelen knew that they were running out of time.

And then, just as they were about to set off, a sudden, searing pain shot through Kaelen's mind, forcing him to his knees as a vision overtook him. The world around him dissolved into darkness, the sound of Alyssa's voice fading into the distance as he was pulled into the depths of his own consciousness.

In the vision, Kaelen saw the Nexus Crystal, its radiant light pulsing with a power that was both awe-inspiring and terrifying. There was something else—something hidden within the crystal's light, a shadow that flickered at the edges of his vision.

And then he saw it—a figure shrouded in darkness, its face obscured but its presence unmistakable. It was the Shadow Keeper, and he was not alone.

Kaelen's heart raced as he realized the truth—the Shadow Keeper was not merely seeking the Nexus Crystal; he was connected to it in a way that Kaelen had not fully understood until now. The crystal was both the source of his power and the key to his downfall.

The vision shifted, and Kaelen saw himself standing at the edge of a vast chasm, the Nexus Crystal hovering before him. The Shadow Keeper stood on the other side, his eyes locked on

Kaelen's as the chasm between them widened, the darkness threatening to consume them both.

And then, with a final, jarring shock, the vision ended, and Kaelen was thrust back into reality, gasping for breath as the pain in his mind subsided.

Alyssa was beside him, her hand on his shoulder, her expression filled with concern. "Kaelen, what happened? Are you alright?"

Kaelen shook his head, trying to make sense of what he had just seen. "The Nexus Crystal… it's connected to the Shadow Keeper. He's not just after it—he's a part of it."

Alyssa's eyes widened in shock, but there was no time to dwell on the revelation. The vision had made one thing clear—they were running out of time, and the final confrontation with the Shadow Keeper was closer than ever.

"We need to move," Kaelen said, his voice filled with both urgency and determination. "We have to reach the temple before it's too late."

Alyssa nodded; her expression steely as she helped Kaelen to his feet. "Let's finish this."

With renewed determination, they set off toward the final location, the coordinates that would lead them to the Nexus Crystal and the showdown that would determine the fate of the timeline. The path ahead was fraught with danger, but they were ready.

Together, they would face whatever challenges lay ahead, determined to protect the future from the darkness that threatened to consume it.

And as they moved through the night, the light of the Nexus Crystal guiding their way, Kaelen knew that they were closer than ever to the final battle that would decide the fate of all time.

Chapter 13

The air around the Temple of Time was thick with tension, each breath heavy as Kaelen and Alyssa approached the ancient structure. The temple, nestled deep within a remote mountain range, was a sight to behold—a colossal edifice carved from dark stone, its surface etched with symbols that seemed to pulse faintly in the fading light. The peaks surrounding it were jagged and imposing, as if nature itself was conspiring to keep the temple hidden from the world.

Kaelen could feel the energy of the Nexus Crystal resonating within the temple, though it was distant, muted. The temporal field surrounding the temple was unstable, causing time to behave unpredictably. One moment, it felt as though hours had passed since they began their approach; the next, it seemed as though they had only just arrived. It was disorienting, but Kaelen knew they couldn't afford to hesitate.

"This is it," Kaelen said, his voice steady despite the apprehension gnawing at him. "The Temple of Time."

Alyssa nodded, her eyes scanning the massive structure. "It feels different here. Like time doesn't move the way it should."

"It's the influence of the Nexus Crystal," Kaelen replied. "The energy is distorting the flow of time. We'll need to stay sharp."

They approached the temple's entrance, a massive archway flanked by two stone statues of ancient, armored figures. The statues' eyes seemed to follow them as they moved, their presence both imposing and unsettling. Kaelen felt a chill run down his spine, but he forced himself to push forward.

The entrance led into a dark corridor; the walls lined with more of the strange symbols that adorned the exterior of the temple. The air inside was cool and still, the silence only broken by the faint echo of their footsteps. As they moved deeper into the temple, the light from outside began to fade, replaced by a soft, eerie glow emanating from the walls themselves.

Kaelen could feel the gauntlet on his arm reacting to the energy in the temple, the device pulsing in time with the faint hum that seemed to reverberate through the stone. It was as if the very structure of the temple was alive, aware of their presence.

"We need to be careful," Kaelen said, his voice low. "This place is filled with traps and trials. The temple was designed to protect the Nexus Crystal, and it won't let us reach it easily."

Alyssa nodded, her expression serious. "We've come this far. Whatever this temple throws at us, we'll face it together."

They continued down the corridor, the path ahead twisting and turning as the temple seemed to shift around them. The first trial came in the form of a series of massive stone doors, each one covered in intricate carvings. As they approached the first door, Kaelen felt a surge of energy from the gauntlet, the symbols on the door beginning to glow.

"This must be one of the trials," Kaelen said, studying the door. "It's a puzzle, a test to see if we're worthy."

Alyssa stepped forward, her eyes narrowing as she examined the carvings. "These symbols... they're similar to the ones we saw in the Nexus Shrine. They represent different points in time, different events."

Kaelen nodded, his mind racing as he tried to decipher the pattern. "We need to match the events in the correct order. The door won't open unless we solve the puzzle."

They worked together, carefully studying the symbols and rearranging them in the correct sequence. The process was slow and meticulous, each symbol requiring careful consideration. As they placed the final symbol in position, the door rumbled, slowly sliding open to reveal the path ahead.

"That's one down," Kaelen said, his voice filled with both relief and determination. "But there will be more."

The corridor beyond the door was darker, the walls closing in around them as they moved deeper into the temple. The air grew colder, and Kaelen could feel the weight of the Shadow Keeper's influence pressing down on them. The environment began to warp, time distorting in strange and unsettling ways. Moments stretched into what felt like hours, while others passed in the blink of an eye.

"It's getting stronger," Alyssa said, her voice tense. "The Shadow Keeper's influence. He's trying to break us down."

Kaelen felt the pressure too, the dark energy gnawing at the edges of his mind. He couldn't let it consume him. He had to stay focused, to push forward, no matter what the temple threw at them.

The next trial was even more treacherous—a series of shifting platforms suspended over a seemingly bottomless pit. The platforms moved in erratic patterns, each one appearing and disappearing at random intervals. The slightest misstep would send them plummeting into the darkness below.

"We have to time this perfectly," Kaelen said, studying the movement of the platforms. "If we're off by even a second..."

Alyssa didn't need him to finish the sentence. She understood the stakes all too well. "We'll go together. Stay close."

They waited for the right moment, watching the platforms intently. When Kaelen finally saw an opening, he nodded to Alyssa, and they leaped onto the first platform. The ground beneath them wobbled slightly, but they kept their balance, quickly moving to the next platform as it appeared.

The journey across the platforms was harrowing, each step a calculated risk. Kaelen could feel the gauntlet's power surging as he used it to create brief stabilizations in the temporal field, slowing the platforms' movement just enough to give them a chance to jump safely. The strain was immense, and Kaelen could feel the toll it was taking on him.

As they reached the final platform, the ground beneath them began to tremble violently, the entire temple shaking as if in response to their progress. Kaelen and Alyssa barely made it to solid ground before the platforms collapsed into the abyss behind them.

"That was too close," Alyssa said, her breath coming in short gasps.

Kaelen nodded, though his mind was already focused on the next challenge. "We're getting closer. The temple is reacting to us—it knows we're near the inner sanctum."

They pressed on, the corridor ahead narrowing into a tight, spiraling staircase that seemed to go on forever. The air grew thicker, the weight of the Shadow Keeper's influence more oppressive with each step. Kaelen could feel his mind starting to slip, the edges of reality blurring as the temporal distortions grew more severe.

Alyssa was there, her presence a steadying force that kept him grounded. She reached out, placing a hand on his arm, her touch warm and reassuring. "We're almost there, Kaelen. Stay with me."

Kaelen nodded, taking a deep breath as he forced himself to focus. They couldn't afford to falter now, not when they were so close.

The staircase finally led them to a massive, circular chamber, the walls lined with ancient runes that glowed faintly in the dim light. At the center of the chamber was a raised platform, and above it, suspended in a field of temporal energy, was a massive, ornate door. This was the final barrier—the entrance to the inner sanctum where the Nexus Crystal was hidden.

As they approached the platform, the temperature in the chamber plummeted, and a dark, oppressive presence filled the air. The shadows along the walls seemed to come alive, coalescing into a figure that materialized in front of them—the Shadow Keeper.

His form was wreathed in darkness, his features obscured by a swirling mass of shadow. Only his eyes were visible, burning with a malevolent light that sent a chill down Kaelen's spine.

"You've come far," the Shadow Keeper said, his voice echoing through the chamber. "But this is where your journey ends."

Kaelen and Alyssa tensed, their senses on high alert as the Shadow Keeper's presence grew stronger. The gauntlet on Kaelen's arm pulsed with energy, responding to the threat as if preparing for the battle to come.

"You can't stop us," Kaelen said, his voice steady despite the fear that gnawed at him. "We're going to find the Nexus Crystal."

The Shadow Keeper's laugh was low and menacing. "The crystal is beyond your reach. It was never meant for you. But you've served your purpose, Kaelen Mercer. You've led me right to it."

Kaelen's heart raced as he realized the truth—the Shadow Keeper had been manipulating them all along, using their quest to bring him closer to the crystal. Even as the realization hit him,

Kaelen knew they couldn't back down. They had to fight, no matter the odds.

The chamber erupted into chaos as the Shadow Keeper attacked, his dark energy filling the air with an oppressive weight that threatened to crush them. Kaelen moved quickly, using the gauntlet to create temporal shields and distortions, deflecting the Shadow Keeper's attacks as he and Alyssa fought to stay on their feet.

The battle was intense, the chamber shaking with the force of their confrontation. Kaelen could feel the strain of the gauntlet's power, the energy within it fluctuating wildly as he pushed it to its limits. The Shadow Keeper's attacks were relentless, his power overwhelming as he sought to crush their resistance.

Kaelen refused to give in. He fought with everything he had, drawing on the gauntlet's power to create temporal shockwaves that threw the Shadow Keeper off balance. Alyssa was by his side, her movements swift and precise as she struck at the Shadow Keeper with a determination that matched Kaelen's own.

As the battle raged on, Kaelen felt a sudden surge of energy from the gauntlet, a final burst of power that flooded his senses. The runes on the walls began to glow brighter, the chamber filling with a blinding light as the temporal energy reached its peak.

And then, just as the light threatened to overwhelm them, Kaelen and Alyssa were thrown back, their bodies hitting the cold stone floor with a jarring impact. The light faded, and the Shadow Keeper's presence vanished as suddenly as it had appeared, leaving them alone in the chamber.

Kaelen groaned as he pushed himself to his feet, his body aching from the battle. Alyssa was beside him, her breath coming in ragged gasps as she looked around the chamber.

"What happened?" she asked, her voice filled with confusion.

Kaelen shook his head, trying to make sense of what they had just experienced. "The temple... it rejected us. It won't let us reach the crystal."

Alyssa's eyes widened in shock. "Then what do we do now?"

Before Kaelen could answer, he noticed something glowing faintly on the platform where the ornate door had been. It was a small, ancient scroll, its surface covered in the same runes that lined the walls of the chamber.

Kaelen approached the scroll cautiously, picking it up and unrolling it. The runes glowed softly in the dim light, the energy within them resonating with the gauntlet on his arm.

"It's a message," Kaelen said, his voice filled with both awe and realization. "A clue to the crystal's true location."

Alyssa stepped closer, her eyes scanning the runes. "So, the crystal isn't here?"

Kaelen nodded, the weight of the revelation settling over him. "The crystal was never here. The temple was a test, a way to see if we were worthy of the knowledge it holds. This scroll… it's the key to finding the real location of the Nexus Crystal."

Alyssa's expression hardened with determination. "Then we're not done yet. We'll follow the clues, find the crystal, and stop the Shadow Keeper."

Kaelen agreed, though the realization that their journey was far from over weighed heavily on him. They had come so close, only to find that the real challenge still lay ahead. They couldn't give up—not now.

As they made their way back through the temple, the air around them began to calm, the temporal distortions fading as the energy within the temple stabilized. The trials they had faced were behind them, but the road ahead would be even more dangerous.

They emerged from the temple into the cool night air, the stars twinkling faintly in the sky above. Kaelen looked out over the landscape; his mind filled with the enormity of the task before them.

"We'll need to be ready," Kaelen said, his voice filled with quiet resolve. "The Shadow Keeper won't stop until he has the crystal, and neither can we."

Alyssa nodded; her expression determined. "We'll find it, Kaelen. We'll stop him."

Together, they set off into the night, the scroll in Kaelen's hand guiding their way. The temple had tested their resolve, but it had also given them the knowledge they needed to continue their quest.

The Nexus Crystal was still out there, hidden in the folds of time, and they were closer than ever to finding it. The Shadow Keeper's power was growing, and the challenges ahead would be greater than anything they had faced before.

As they disappeared into the darkness, Kaelen felt a deep sense of purpose settle over him. The journey was far from over, but he knew they would face whatever came next with strength and determination.

For now, the crystal remained hidden, but the path to it was clear. And Kaelen and Alyssa would follow that path, no matter where it led.

Chapter 14

The wind howled through the mountains, carrying with it the sharp bite of cold as Kaelen and Alyssa made their way down the narrow path leading away from the Temple of Time. The stars above were obscured by thick clouds, casting the world around them in darkness save for the soft glow of the gauntlet on Kaelen's arm. The revelation from the temple weighed heavily on both of them, the ancient scroll now tucked safely in Kaelen's pack, but its implications lingered in their minds like an ever-present shadow.

They walked in silence for a time, the only sounds the crunch of gravel beneath their boots and the distant echoes of the wind through the valleys below. The journey from the temple had been fraught with danger, and now, as they ventured further into the unknown, the weight of their mission seemed to grow with each passing step.

Finally, Alyssa broke the silence, her voice subdued but steady. "That scroll... it changes everything. The Nexus Crystal isn't where we thought it was. We're further from our goal than we realized."

Kaelen nodded, though his eyes remained fixed on the path ahead. "The crystal was never at the Temple of Time. It was a test, a way to see if we were worthy of the knowledge it holds. Now that we know where it's truly hidden... it feels like we've only scratched the surface of what's to come."

Alyssa glanced at him, her expression thoughtful. "Do you think we're ready? For whatever comes next?"

Kaelen paused, considering her question. The journey had already tested them in ways he hadn't anticipated—physically, mentally, and emotionally. They had faced the Shadow Keeper's minions, navigated treacherous landscapes, and uncovered secrets that had been buried for centuries. The path ahead promised to be even more perilous, with challenges they couldn't yet foresee.

"I don't know if anyone can ever be truly ready for something like this," Kaelen admitted. "But we don't have a choice. We've come too far to turn back now."

Alyssa nodded, her expression resolute. "Then we keep moving forward. We'll find the crystal, no matter what it takes."

They continued their descent, the path winding through the mountainside, growing narrower and more precarious with each step. The terrain was treacherous, the rocks slick with moisture from the mist that clung to the peaks. Despite the physical challenge, Kaelen's mind was preoccupied with the scroll and the information it contained.

The scroll had revealed a new location—an ancient site hidden deep within a forgotten corner of the world. The journey to reach it would be long and arduous, taking them through uncharted territory filled with dangers both natural and temporal. It was their only lead, the key to finding the Nexus Crystal and stopping the Shadow Keeper's plans.

As they pressed on, Kaelen began to notice something strange. At first, it was subtle—just a flicker at the edge of his vision, a fleeting sense of déjà vu that made him question his surroundings. As they moved deeper into the mountains, the sensation grew stronger, more insistent, until it became impossible to ignore.

"Do you feel that?" Kaelen asked, his voice tinged with unease.

Alyssa looked at him, her brow furrowed. "Feel what?"

Kaelen hesitated, searching for the right words. "It's like... echoes. Echoes of something that's already happened, or maybe something that's about to happen. I can't explain it, but it's as if the past is bleeding into the present."

Alyssa's eyes widened slightly, her hand instinctively going to her weapon. "Is it the Shadow Keeper? Is he trying to manipulate us again?"

Kaelen shook his head. "No, this feels different. It's not an attack, more like... a memory. But not mine. It's like I'm seeing things through someone else's eyes."

They continued walking, and soon, the flickers began to take shape. The world around them seemed to shift and warp, the rocks and trees blurring as if viewed through a pane of distorted glass. And then, suddenly, they were no longer alone.

Kaelen blinked, and for a moment, he saw a group of figures moving through the same mountainside—a vision of the past, a memory from another time. The figures were dressed in ancient armor, their faces obscured by helmets adorned with the same symbols they had seen in the Temple of Time. They moved with purpose, their expressions grim, as if they too were on a mission of great importance.

One of the figures paused, turning to look directly at Kaelen, their eyes meeting his with a startling intensity. Kaelen felt a jolt of recognition, though he had never seen this person before. It was as if he were looking into a mirror, seeing a reflection of himself from a time long forgotten.

And then, just as quickly as it had appeared, the vision faded, the figures dissolving into the mist as the present reasserted itself. Kaelen staggered, his hand reaching out to steady himself against a nearby rock.

"Kaelen!" Alyssa's voice was filled with concern as she moved to support him. "What happened? What did you see?"

Kaelen shook his head, trying to clear the lingering effects of the vision. "I saw... people. From another time. They were here, in this exact spot. It was like I was seeing a memory, but it wasn't mine."

Alyssa's expression grew more serious. "The Nexus Crystal's influence must be stronger than we realized. If it's causing these kinds of temporal echoes, it means we're getting closer to something powerful—something that's been hidden for a long time."

Kaelen nodded, though the experience had left him shaken. The visions were more than just echoes of the past—they felt like a warning, a glimpse of the dangers that lay ahead. They couldn't afford to turn back now. They had to press on, no matter what awaited them.

They continued their journey, the path growing steeper as they descended into a deep valley. The mist thickened, swirling around them like a living entity, and the temperature dropped, the air growing colder with each step. The landscape was bleak and desolate, the remnants of ancient ruins jutting out from the ground like the bones of some long-dead giant.

As they walked, they passed the remains of old battles— rusted weapons, broken shields, and the skeletal remains of warriors who had fallen long ago. The sight was a grim reminder of the timeline's fragility, and the countless lives that had been lost in the pursuit of power.

Kaelen paused beside one of the skeletons, his gaze lingering on the tattered remnants of armor that still clung to the bones. The symbols etched into the metal were the same as those they had seen in the temple, a clear sign that these warriors had once been connected to the Nexus Crystal in some way.

"It's all connected," Kaelen murmured, more to himself than to Alyssa. "The temple, the crystal, these ruins... they're all pieces of the same puzzle."

Alyssa knelt beside him, her eyes scanning the skeletal remains. "These people died protecting something. Maybe they were guardians, like the Time Keepers."

Kaelen nodded, though the thought only deepened the sense of unease that had settled over him. If these warriors had fallen in the defense of the Nexus Crystal, what chance did they have of succeeding where so many others had failed?

He couldn't afford to dwell on those thoughts. The path ahead was clear, and they had to keep moving.

As they ventured deeper into the valley, the echoes of the past grew stronger. Kaelen began to see more visions—fleeting glimpses of battles long past, of warriors locked in combat, of ancient rituals performed in the shadow of massive stone monuments. The visions were disorienting, leaving him with a sense of unease that was impossible to shake.

Through it all, Kaelen felt a strange sense of connection to the past, as if the timeline itself was trying to communicate with him. The visions offered hints, clues that seemed to guide their path, leading them deeper into the heart of the valley.

And then, as they rounded a bend in the path, they saw it—a figure standing alone in the mist, their form shrouded in shadow. The figure was tall and imposing, their presence radiating a quiet power that immediately set Kaelen and Alyssa on edge.

Kaelen's hand went to the gauntlet, the device pulsing with energy as he prepared for a confrontation. The figure made no move to attack, instead remaining still, as if waiting for them to approach.

"Who are you?" Kaelen called out, his voice steady but cautious.

The figure remained silent for a moment, and then they spoke, their voice calm and measured. "I am a guardian of the timeline, a watcher of the past and the future. You have come far, Kaelen Mercer, but your journey is not yet complete."

Kaelen exchanged a glance with Alyssa, both of them on high alert. "What do you want?"

The figure stepped forward, the mist parting around them to reveal a face that was both ancient and ageless, with eyes that seemed to hold the weight of countless years. "It is not what I want, but what you seek. The Nexus Crystal holds the power to shape the timeline, to alter the course of history itself. But such power comes at a great cost."

Kaelen felt a chill run down his spine at the figure's words. "What cost?"

The figure's gaze was piercing, as if they were looking into the very depths of Kaelen's soul. "The crystal is not just an artifact—it is a living embodiment of time itself. To wield its power is to take on a responsibility that few can bear. The path you have chosen is fraught with danger, and the consequences of failure are dire."

Alyssa stepped forward, her voice firm. "We understand the risks. We're prepared to do whatever it takes to protect the timeline."

The figure nodded, though their expression remained inscrutable. "Your resolve is commendable but be warned—there are forces at play that even you cannot fully comprehend. The Shadow Keeper's influence grows stronger with each passing moment, and he will stop at nothing to claim the crystal for himself."

Kaelen's grip tightened on the gauntlet. "We won't let that happen."

The figure's gaze softened, though the intensity in their eyes remained. "There is one final trial you must face before you can continue your journey. A test of your resolve, your strength, and your ability to see the truth that lies beyond the veil of time."

Kaelen felt a knot of tension form in his chest, but he nodded. "What do we need to do?"

The figure raised a hand, and the mist around them began to swirl and shift, forming a doorway of light that pulsed with a strange, otherworldly energy. "Enter the passage, and you will find your answer. But know this—the path you take from here will determine not only your fate, but the fate of the timeline itself."

Kaelen exchanged another glance with Alyssa, her expression mirroring the resolve he felt within himself. They had come too far to turn back now, and whatever trial awaited them, they would face it together.

With a deep breath, Kaelen stepped forward, leading Alyssa through the doorway of light. The mist closed around them, and for a moment, the world seemed to dissolve into nothingness. And then, as suddenly as it had begun, the sensation passed, and they found themselves standing in a vast, empty space, the ground beneath their feet glowing faintly with a soft, ethereal light.

The space was both infinite and confined, a paradoxical void that defied explanation. And yet, at the center of it all, Kaelen saw a figure—a reflection of himself, dressed in the ancient armor of the warriors from his visions.

The figure stepped forward, its movements mirroring Kaelen's own, as if it were a shadow of his past. "This is your final trial," the figure said, its voice echoing through the void. "To prove that you are worthy of the knowledge you seek, you must face yourself—the truth of who you are, and the choices that have brought you here."

Kaelen felt a surge of emotions—fear, uncertainty, determination—all mingling together in a maelstrom within him. He couldn't hesitate now. He had to face whatever lay ahead, to confront the shadows of his past and emerge stronger for it.

As the figure raised its weapon, Kaelen felt the gauntlet pulse with energy, the power within it responding to the challenge. He glanced at Alyssa, her expression filled with both concern and encouragement.

"Whatever happens," Kaelen said, his voice steady, "we face it together."

Alyssa nodded, her eyes meeting his with unwavering resolve. "Together."

The final trial had begun, and Kaelen knew that the outcome would determine the course of their journey—and the fate of the timeline itself.

Chapter 15

The space around Kaelen and Alyssa was vast and disorienting, an endless expanse of shimmering light that seemed to pulse with the rhythm of a heartbeat. The ground beneath their feet was solid but translucent, reflecting a distorted image of the world above. Everything in this place felt surreal, as though they had stepped into a realm that existed outside the boundaries of time and reality.

Kaelen tightened his grip on the gauntlet, feeling its power hum against his skin. The figure that stood before him— his mirror image—remained motionless, its expression unreadable. The silence between them was heavy, charged with a tension that threatened to snap at any moment.

"This is your final trial," the mirror image said, its voice echoing through the void. It was Kaelen's voice, yet there was something colder, more distant about it. "To prove that you are worthy of the knowledge you seek, you must face yourself—the truth of who you are, and the choices that have brought you here."

Kaelen swallowed hard, his mind racing. He had faced countless dangers on this journey—battles against powerful enemies, treacherous landscapes, and the ever-present threat of the Shadow Keeper. But this... this was different. This was a battle within himself, against the doubts and fears that had lingered in the shadows of his mind for so long.

Alyssa stood beside him, her eyes filled with concern as she looked between Kaelen and his reflection. "You don't have to do this alone," she said, her voice soft but firm. "I'm here with you."

Kaelen nodded, grateful for her presence, but he knew that this was a battle only he could fight. The reflection was a manifestation of everything he had tried to suppress—the guilt over his brother's death, the fear of becoming like the Shadow Keeper, the doubt that he was worthy of the power he wielded.

With a deep breath, Kaelen stepped forward, meeting the reflection's gaze. "I'm ready."

The reflection's lips curled into a cold smile, and then, without warning, it lunged forward, its movements a mirror image of Kaelen's own. Kaelen barely had time to react, raising the gauntlet to block the strike as the two of them clashed in a flurry of blows.

It was like fighting himself—every move he made was countered perfectly, every strike met with an equal force. The reflection moved with the same grace and precision as Kaelen, its attacks fluid and relentless. It was as though Kaelen were battling his own shadow, every weakness and strength laid bare.

The clash of their weapons echoed through the void, a cacophony of sound that reverberated in Kaelen's mind. The reflection was relentless, pressing the attack with a ferocity that left Kaelen struggling to keep up. It wasn't just the physical toll that was wearing him down—it was the words that accompanied each strike, the taunts that cut deeper than any blade.

"Do you really think you can control this power?" the reflection sneered; its voice laced with contempt. "You're no different from the Shadow Keeper. You've already started down the same path—using time as a weapon, bending it to your will. How long before you become the very thing you're fighting against?"

Kaelen gritted his teeth, forcing himself to block out the words, to focus on the fight. The reflection's voice was relentless, echoing his deepest fears and insecurities.

"Your brother died because of you," the reflection continued, its tone cruel and unforgiving. "You dragged him into your quest for glory, and now his blood is on your hands. Do you think Elias would be proud of the man you've become? A man who's willing to sacrifice anything and anyone to achieve his goals?"

Kaelen stumbled, the reflection's words hitting him like a physical blow. Memories of Elias flashed through his mind—his brother's laughter, his unwavering support, the way he had always believed in Kaelen, even when Kaelen didn't believe in himself. And then, the memory of that fateful day—the day Elias had died, and Kaelen had been powerless to save him.

The reflection's smile widened, sensing Kaelen's turmoil. "You've already failed the people you care about. How long before you fail Alyssa too? How long before she becomes another casualty of your obsession?"

Kaelen's heart clenched at the thought. Alyssa had been by his side through everything, her unwavering support giving him the strength to keep going. The idea of losing her, of failing her in the same way he had failed Elias, was more than he could bear.

The reflection struck again, its blade slicing through the air with deadly precision. Kaelen barely managed to deflect the blow, his movements growing sluggish under the weight of his doubts. He could feel himself weakening, the fight slipping away from him as the reflection's words burrowed deeper into his mind.

Then, through the haze of fear and self-doubt, Kaelen heard another voice—Alyssa's voice, clear and strong, cutting through the darkness like a beacon of light.

"Kaelen, don't listen to it!" Alyssa called out; her voice filled with determination. "This isn't who you are! You're stronger than this!"

Kaelen's grip on the gauntlet tightened, Alyssa's words grounding him, pulling him back from the brink. She was right—this wasn't who he was. He wasn't the man the reflection was trying to make him believe he was. He wasn't a failure, and he wasn't destined to become the Shadow Keeper. He was Kaelen Mercer, and he had the power to choose his own path.

With a surge of resolve, Kaelen pushed back against the reflection, forcing it to retreat. The reflection's smile faltered, its movements becoming more erratic as Kaelen began to regain control. The taunts continued, but Kaelen no longer let them affect him. He knew who he was, and he knew what he had to do.

The turning point came when the reflection attempted to exploit Kaelen's most painful memory—the moment Elias had died. The reflection conjured the image of Elias, his face twisted in pain and betrayal as he reached out to Kaelen with a bloodied hand.

"Why didn't you save me, Kaelen?" the reflection taunted, using Elias's voice. "You were supposed to protect me. You promised."

For a moment, the sight of Elias's dying form threatened to break Kaelen's resolve. The guilt, the grief—it all came rushing back, threatening to overwhelm him. Then he remembered Alyssa's words, the strength in her voice, the way she had always believed in him.

Kaelen took a deep breath, focusing on the memory of Elias not as a source of pain, but as a source of strength. Elias had believed in him, had trusted him, and Kaelen knew that his brother wouldn't want him to be consumed by guilt. Elias would want him to fight, to keep going, to make sure that his death hadn't been in vain.

With that thought, Kaelen turned the memory on its head, using it to fuel his resolve rather than weaken it. He met the reflection's gaze, his eyes burning with determination.

"Elias's death wasn't my fault," Kaelen said, his voice steady. "I did everything I could to save him. And I won't let his memory be used against me."

The reflection's form began to waver, its smile twisting into a snarl as it realized that its hold on Kaelen was slipping. "You're lying to yourself," it hissed, its voice losing some of its power. "You're weak, just like before. You'll fail again."

"No," Kaelen replied, his voice filled with conviction. "I'm stronger now. I've learned from my mistakes, and I won't let them define me."

With a final surge of strength, Kaelen raised the gauntlet, channeling its power into a concentrated burst of energy. The light from the gauntlet blazed brightly, illuminating the void as it shot toward the reflection.

The reflection tried to counter, raising its own weapon, but it was too late. The burst of energy struck the reflection head-on, shattering it into a million shards of light. The void around them trembled, the distorted reflections of the world above rippling and then fading away as the trial chamber began to dissolve.

Kaelen fell to his knees, the adrenaline of the fight draining away to be replaced by a deep, bone-weary exhaustion. His chest heaved as he struggled to catch his breath, the remnants of the battle still echoing in his mind.

Alyssa was at his side in an instant, her hands gentle as she helped him back to his feet. "Kaelen, are you alright?"

Kaelen nodded, though his legs felt unsteady beneath him. "I'm okay," he said, though his voice was hoarse from the effort. "It's over. I beat it."

Alyssa's eyes were filled with a mix of relief and admiration as she looked at him. "You did it. You beat the trial."

Kaelen managed a small smile, though it was tinged with weariness. "I couldn't have done it without you."

Alyssa shook her head. "You did the hard part. I was just here to remind you of who you really are."

Kaelen squeezed her hand, grateful beyond words for her support. The trial had been grueling, pushing him to the very edge of his limits, he had come out the other side stronger and more certain of himself.

The space around them continued to shift, the ethereal light fading as the trial chamber dissolved completely. Kaelen and Alyssa found themselves back in the mist-covered valley, the mysterious figure who had guided them here standing at a distance, watching them with a calm, unreadable expression.

"You have passed the trial," the figure said, their voice carrying a note of approval. "You have faced your own darkness and emerged victorious. The knowledge you seek is now within your grasp."

Kaelen met the figure's gaze, feeling a renewed sense of purpose settle over him. "What do we need to do next?"

The figure gestured toward the path that lay ahead, the mist parting to reveal the continuation of their journey. "The path forward will be fraught with danger, but you are ready. The Nexus Crystal is within reach, but it will require all of your strength, your courage, and your resolve to claim it."

Alyssa nodded, her expression resolute. "We're ready."

The figure inclined their head, a gesture of respect. "Then go, Kaelen Mercer. Your destiny awaits."

With a final glance at the figure, Kaelen and Alyssa turned and began walking down the path, the mist closing behind them as they moved forward. The weight of the trial still lingered in Kaelen's mind, but it no longer felt like a burden. It was a reminder of the journey they had undertaken, the challenges they had faced, and the strength they had found in themselves and in each other.

As they walked, Kaelen felt a sense of clarity that had eluded him for so long. The doubts and fears that had plagued him were still there, but they no longer held the same power over him. He had faced them, confronted the darkest parts of himself, and come out stronger on the other side.

The path ahead was long, and the challenges were far from over. For the first time, Kaelen felt truly ready to face whatever lay ahead. With Alyssa by his side, he knew they could overcome anything.

The Nexus Crystal was still out there, waiting for them. And together, they would find it, no matter the cost.

Chapter 16

The air grew colder as Kaelen and Alyssa pressed onward, the path before them narrowing into a treacherous trail that wound through jagged cliffs and dense forests. The sun was hidden behind a blanket of thick, gray clouds, casting the world in a perpetual twilight that seemed to blur the boundaries between day and night. The atmosphere was oppressive, heavy with the promise of a storm, and every step felt like a battle against the weight of the journey ahead.

Kaelen kept his eyes on the path, his senses on high alert for any sign of danger. The landscape around them had grown increasingly hostile since they left the trial chamber, as if the very world was conspiring against their progress. Rocks crumbled beneath their feet, the ground threatening to give way with each step, and the wind howled through the narrow valleys, carrying with it the chill of impending disaster.

Alyssa moved beside him; her face set in a determined expression as she navigated the rocky terrain. The silence between them was comfortable, a shared understanding of the gravity of their mission. The trial Kaelen had faced had shaken them both, but it had also strengthened their resolve. They were in this together, and no matter what challenges lay ahead, they would face them side by side.

As they rounded a bend in the path, the wind suddenly picked up, whipping through the trees with a force that sent leaves and debris flying into the air. The sky darkened further, the clouds above churning with ominous energy. Kaelen felt a shiver run down his spine as the first drops of rain began to fall, quickly turning into a torrential downpour that soaked them to the bone.

"We need to find shelter," Kaelen shouted over the roar of the wind, his voice barely audible above the storm.

Alyssa nodded, her eyes scanning the landscape for any sign of cover. They were high in the mountains now, the path winding precariously along the edge of a steep cliff. The storm made the journey even more dangerous, the ground slick with rain and the visibility reduced to almost nothing.

"There!" Alyssa pointed ahead, where the outline of a large, overhanging rock offered some protection from the elements. They hurried toward it, the wind pushing against them as they struggled to stay upright on the slippery path.

By the time they reached the shelter, both Kaelen and Alyssa were drenched, their clothes clinging to their bodies and their breaths coming in short, ragged gasps. They huddled beneath the overhang, grateful for even the minimal protection it provided from the storm.

Kaelen leaned against the rock, his chest heaving as he tried to catch his breath. "This storm... it's not natural."

Alyssa nodded, wiping rain from her face. "The Shadow Keeper's influence is growing stronger. We've seen what he can do to the timeline—this storm is just another sign that he's gaining power."

Kaelen's thoughts drifted back to the strange temporal distortions they had encountered on their journey—time loops, sudden shifts in reality, moments that seemed to stretch into infinity or vanish in the blink of an eye. It was as if the very fabric of time was unraveling around them, the Shadow Keeper's presence warping everything it touched.

"We need to keep moving," Kaelen said, though the storm showed no signs of letting up. "The longer we stay here, the more vulnerable we are."

Alyssa glanced out at the storm, her eyes narrowing in determination. "Agreed. But we need to be careful. The path ahead will be even more treacherous in this weather."

They waited for a brief lull in the storm before stepping back onto the path, their movements cautious as they navigated the slippery rocks. The wind whipped around them, tearing at their clothes and making it difficult to see more than a few feet ahead. The rain pounded against them, turning the path into a muddy, treacherous slope that threatened to send them plummeting into the abyss below.

They pressed on, driven by the knowledge that every moment they delayed brought the Shadow Keeper closer to his goal. The Nexus Crystal was still out there, waiting for them to find it, and they couldn't afford to let anything stand in their way.

As they climbed higher into the mountains, the storm grew more intense, the wind howling with a fury that shook the very ground beneath their feet. Lightning flashed in the distance, illuminating the jagged peaks for a brief moment before plunging the world back into darkness.

Kaelen's muscles ached with the effort of the climb, each step a battle against the elements and the unforgiving terrain. He forced himself to keep going, his determination fueled by the memory of the trial he had faced—the reflection of his fears and doubts that had nearly broken him. He had overcome that challenge, and he would overcome this one too.

Alyssa was a steady presence beside him, her movements sure and confident despite the treacherous conditions. Her strength and resilience were a constant source of support, reminding Kaelen that he wasn't alone in this fight. They were a team, and together, they could face whatever the Shadow Keeper threw at them.

As they crested the next rise, the storm seemed to reach a new level of intensity, the wind howling like a living thing, and the rain coming down in sheets that made it almost impossible to see. Through the chaos, Kaelen caught sight of something that made his heart skip a beat.

A figure stood on the path ahead, silhouetted against the storm. The figure was tall and imposing, their features obscured by the darkness and the driving rain. There was something about the way they stood, the air of calm confidence that surrounded them, that set Kaelen on edge.

Alyssa noticed the figure at the same time, her hand instinctively going to her weapon. "Who's there?" she called out, her voice sharp with suspicion.

The figure remained silent for a moment, and then they began to move forward, their steps slow and deliberate. As they drew closer, the storm seemed to calm around them, the wind dying down and the rain lessening, as if the very elements were bending to their will.

When the figure was close enough for Kaelen to see their face, he felt a jolt of recognition, though he couldn't place where he had seen them before. The figure was a man, his features sharp and angular, with eyes that seemed to gleam with an inner light. He wore a cloak that billowed around him, despite the now-gentle breeze, and there was an air of authority about him that made Kaelen wary.

"Who are you?" Kaelen asked, his voice cautious but firm.

The man smiled, though the expression didn't reach his eyes. "A friend, perhaps. Or an enemy, depending on how you choose to see me."

Alyssa narrowed her eyes, her grip on her weapon tightening. "What do you want?"

The man's gaze flicked to Alyssa, then back to Kaelen. "I come with a warning," he said, his tone even. "The path you are on is a dangerous one, fraught with peril at every turn. The Shadow Keeper is closer than you think, and his power grows with each passing moment. If you continue on this path, you may find yourself walking straight into his trap."

Kaelen exchanged a glance with Alyssa, uncertainty flickering in his eyes. "How do you know this? Who are you, really?"

The man's smile widened, but there was no warmth in it. "My identity is of little consequence. What matters is that I have knowledge that can aid you, if you are willing to listen."

Alyssa's eyes flashed with suspicion. "Why should we trust you?"

The man shrugged, the movement casual. "Trust is a rare commodity in these times, I understand. But consider this—if I were your enemy, would I not have already struck you down? I offer you information that may save your lives, nothing more."

Kaelen felt a sense of unease settle over him, but he knew they couldn't afford to ignore the possibility that this man's words held some truth. "What is it you're offering?"

The man's gaze grew more intense, as if he were weighing his words carefully. "There is a place, not far from here—a temple, ancient and forgotten by most. It is said that within this temple lies a relic, a fragment of the Nexus Crystal's power. The Shadow Keeper seeks it, and if he finds it before you do, the consequences will be dire."

Kaelen's heart raced at the mention of the Nexus Crystal, but he forced himself to remain cautious. "And you're telling us this out of the goodness of your heart?"

The man's smile returned, though it remained as enigmatic as ever. "Let us say that our goals are temporarily aligned. I do not wish to see the timeline fall into chaos any more than you do. Consider my warning and make your choice. But know this—time is running out."

With that, the man turned and began to walk away, his form gradually fading into the storm until he was gone, as if he had never been there at all.

Kaelen and Alyssa stood in silence for a moment, the storm still raging around them, though its fury had lessened. Kaelen's mind raced, trying to make sense of the encounter. The man's words had been cryptic, his motives unclear, but there was something about him that suggested he knew more than he was letting on.

"What do you think?" Kaelen asked, turning to Alyssa.

Alyssa's expression was thoughtful, though her eyes still held a trace of suspicion. "He could be leading us into a trap. But if what he said is true, we can't afford to ignore it. The Shadow Keeper finding that relic would be disastrous."

Kaelen nodded; his decision made. "Then we'll go to the temple. But we'll be cautious—this could still be a trick."

Alyssa agreed, and they set off once more, the storm continuing to batter them as they made their way down the treacherous path. The encounter with the mysterious man had left them both on edge, but it had also given them a new sense of urgency. The Shadow Keeper was growing stronger, and the stakes had never been higher.

As they neared the location hinted at by the man, the environment grew even more hostile. The path became almost impossible to navigate, with sheer cliffs on one side and a drop into darkness on the other. The storm showed no signs of letting up, the wind and rain lashing at them with a fury that made every step a challenge.

Through it all, Kaelen and Alyssa pressed on, driven by the knowledge that they were getting closer to their goal. The air around them seemed to hum with energy, the influence of the Nexus Crystal growing stronger with each passing moment. Kaelen could feel it in the gauntlet, the device pulsing with a power that resonated with the storm itself.

And then, just as they reached the top of a particularly steep climb, the storm suddenly stopped. The wind died down, the rain ceased, and the clouds parted to reveal a small, secluded valley nestled between the peaks. At the center of the valley stood a temple—ancient, weathered, and half-buried in the earth, but unmistakably the place the man had described.

246

Kaelen and Alyssa exchanged a glance, their expressions a mix of determination and wariness. They had found the temple, but they knew that their journey was far from over. Whatever lay inside would be the next test of their strength and resolve.

"Are you ready?" Kaelen asked, his voice quiet but steady.

Alyssa nodded; her eyes fixed on the temple ahead. "Let's do this."

With that, they began their descent into the valley, the temple looming before them like a silent sentinel of the past. The path ahead was uncertain, and the dangers were greater than ever, but they were ready to face whatever challenges awaited them.

Together, they would uncover the secrets of the temple, find the relic, and stop the Shadow Keeper before it was too late.

Chapter 17

The temple loomed before Kaelen and Alyssa, an imposing structure of weathered stone that seemed to defy the passage of time. Its walls were covered in intricate carvings, depicting scenes of battles long forgotten, ancient symbols, and the mysterious figures who had once walked its halls. The air was thick with an unspoken power, and every step they took seemed to echo with the weight of history.

Kaelen couldn't shake the feeling of unease that had settled over him since their encounter with the mysterious man. The storm had ceased, but the air was still charged with tension, as if the very atmosphere was holding its breath, waiting for something to happen. He glanced at Alyssa, her expression as resolute as ever, though he could see the same tension mirrored in her eyes.

"We need to be on our guard," Kaelen said quietly as they approached the entrance. The massive stone doors stood ajar, as if inviting them inside, but there was something about the way the darkness seemed to spill out from within that made him hesitate. "This place feels... wrong."

Alyssa nodded, her hand resting on the hilt of her weapon. "The Shadow Keeper might have set traps for us. We can't afford to let our guard down."

With a deep breath, Kaelen stepped forward, the gauntlet on his arm pulsing faintly with energy as they crossed the threshold. The interior of the temple was even more imposing than the exterior, with high ceilings that seemed to stretch into infinity and walls lined with more of the intricate carvings. The light from the gauntlet illuminated the path ahead, casting long, eerie shadows that danced along the stone floor.

They moved cautiously, every sense alert for the slightest sign of danger. The air was cool and still, the only sound the soft echo of their footsteps as they ventured deeper into the temple.

The carvings on the walls seemed to shift and change as they passed, the scenes depicted in them becoming more intense battles fought with weapons of light and shadow, figures wielding immense power, and the unmistakable image of the Nexus Crystal, glowing with an otherworldly light.

"This place was built to protect the crystal," Alyssa murmured, her voice barely above a whisper. "Or what's left of it."

Kaelen nodded, his eyes scanning the carvings for any clues that might help them navigate the temple. "Whatever's in here, it's tied to the crystal's power. We need to be careful."

As they rounded a corner, they were met with the first of the temple's challenges—a massive stone door, covered in symbols that glowed faintly in the dim light. The door was sealed, with no visible means of opening it, but Kaelen could feel the energy radiating from it, a pulse that resonated with the gauntlet on his arm.

"This must be the first trial," Kaelen said, stepping closer to examine the symbols. They were similar to the ones they had encountered in the Nexus Shrine, ancient and complex, with meanings that were difficult to decipher. "It looks like a puzzle. We'll need to solve it to move forward."

Alyssa joined him, her eyes narrowing as she studied the symbols. "These represent different elements—fire, water, earth, and air. They're arranged in a way that doesn't make sense."

Kaelen nodded, his mind already working through the possibilities. "We need to find the correct sequence. If we can align the symbols in the right order, it should unlock the door."

They worked together, carefully shifting the symbols into place, each movement met with a faint hum of energy as the gauntlet responded to the puzzle's power. It was a slow, meticulous process, with each symbol requiring careful consideration and adjustment. Gradually, the pattern began to emerge, the symbols aligning in a sequence that resonated with the energy of the temple.

With a final click, the symbols locked into place, and the stone door rumbled open, revealing the path ahead.

"That's one down," Kaelen said, though he knew there would be more challenges to come. "Let's keep moving."

The corridor beyond the door was narrow, the walls closing in around them as they ventured deeper into the heart of the temple. The air grew colder, and Kaelen could feel the weight of the temple's power pressing down on them, a palpable presence that seemed to pulse in time with the beating of his heart.

As they walked, the carvings on the walls became more chaotic, the scenes depicted in them growing darker and more violent. The figures in the carvings were no longer triumphant warriors, but twisted forms, their faces contorted in agony as they fought against forces that seemed to tear at the very fabric of reality.

"This place isn't just a temple," Alyssa said, her voice filled with a mix of awe and dread. "It's a battleground."

Kaelen felt a shiver run down his spine at her words. The temple had been built to protect the Nexus Crystal, but it had also been the site of a great conflict, a struggle between forces that had left their mark on the very walls. Whatever had happened here, it had been a battle of unimaginable power, and the echoes of that conflict still lingered in the air.

They continued onward; their progress slowed by the increasing complexity of the temple's challenges. More puzzles awaited them—rooms filled with shifting stone blocks, hidden pressure plates that triggered deadly mechanisms, and symbols that required deciphering to unlock the way forward. Each trial was more difficult than the last, testing their intellect, agility, and resolve.

As they ventured deeper, Kaelen began to sense something else—a presence that seemed to watch their every move, a force that was growing stronger the closer they got to the temple's heart.

"The guardian," Kaelen said, the realization hitting him with a sudden clarity. "It's here."

Alyssa's eyes darted around the corridor, her grip on her weapon tightening. "Do you think it knows we're here?"

Kaelen nodded, his voice grim. "It's been watching us since we entered the temple. And I think it's waiting for us."

They pressed on, the atmosphere growing heavier with each step. The carvings on the walls became almost incomprehensible, the images distorted and fractured, as if the power that had created them had begun to unravel. The corridor twisted and turned, leading them deeper into the temple's depths until they finally reached a massive chamber, its walls lined with ancient runes that pulsed with a faint, ominous light.

At the center of the chamber was a pedestal, and on it rested the relic—a fragment of the Nexus Crystal, glowing with a soft, ethereal light. The relic was small, but its power was unmistakable, radiating energy that resonated with the gauntlet on Kaelen's arm.

Kaelen and Alyssa approached the pedestal cautiously, every sense on high alert. The chamber was silent, but the air was thick with tension, as if the very walls were holding their breath.

"We've found it," Kaelen said, his voice filled with a mix of relief and apprehension. "The relic."

Alyssa nodded, her eyes never leaving the glowing fragment. "Where's the guardian?"

As if in response to her words, the chamber suddenly came alive with a surge of energy. The runes on the walls flared with light, and the ground beneath them trembled as a figure materialized at the far end of the chamber.

The guardian was massive, its form a swirling mass of shadows and light, its eyes burning with a cold, calculating intelligence. It was humanoid in shape, but its features were constantly shifting, its body composed of the same energy that radiated from the Nexus Crystal.

Kaelen felt a surge of fear and determination as the guardian advanced toward them, its movements slow and deliberate, as if it was testing them, waiting to see what they would do.

"We have to fight it," Kaelen said, his voice steady despite the fear that gnawed at him. "It's not going to let us take the relic without a fight."

Alyssa nodded, her weapon already drawn, the blade glowing faintly in the dim light. "We've come this far. We're not turning back now."

The guardian paused for a moment, its form shifting as it seemed to assess them. And then, with a sudden burst of speed, it attacked.

Kaelen barely had time to react as the guardian lunged at him, its hand—a mass of swirling energy—slashing toward him with deadly precision. He raised the gauntlet, channeling its power to create a temporal shield that deflected the blow, but the force of the impact sent him staggering back.

Alyssa was quick to strike, her blade slicing through the guardian's form, but the creature barely seemed to notice, its body reforming almost instantly as it turned its attention to her.

The battle was intense, the guardian's attacks relentless and powerful. The very chamber seemed to react to the creature's will, the walls closing in around them, the floor shifting and buckling as the guardian unleashed its fury.

Kaelen used the gauntlet to slow time, giving himself and Alyssa a brief advantage as they tried to find a way to defeat the guardian. The creature was too powerful, its form constantly shifting, making it difficult to land a decisive blow.

"We can't keep this up!" Alyssa shouted over the din of the battle; her voice filled with frustration. "It's too strong!"

Kaelen knew she was right. The guardian was unlike anything they had faced before—an ancient being of pure energy, tied to the power of the Nexus Crystal itself. They couldn't afford to give up. They had come too far, and the relic was their only hope of stopping the Shadow Keeper.

As the guardian lunged at him again, Kaelen felt a sudden surge of energy from the gauntlet, a pulse that resonated with the relic on the pedestal. An idea formed in his mind, a desperate plan that might just give them the edge they needed.

"Alyssa, cover me!" Kaelen shouted; his voice filled with urgency.

Alyssa nodded, throwing herself at the guardian with renewed determination, her strikes aimed at keeping the creature off balance. Kaelen took a deep breath, focusing all of his energy on the gauntlet, channeling its power toward the relic.

The guardian roared in anger as it sensed what Kaelen was doing, its form shifting as it tried to reach him. Alyssa was relentless, her attacks forcing the creature to defend itself, buying Kaelen the time he needed.

With a final surge of power, Kaelen unleashed the energy of the gauntlet, directing it toward the relic. The chamber was filled with a blinding light as the energy connected with the fragment, the power of the Nexus Crystal resonating through the temple.

The guardian let out a piercing scream, its form unraveling as the energy overwhelmed it. The creature's body began to disintegrate, the shadows and light that composed it dissolving into nothingness as it was consumed by the power of the relic.

Kaelen collapsed to his knees as the light faded, his body trembling with exhaustion. The guardian was gone, its presence erased from the chamber, but the battle had taken its toll on him.

Alyssa was at his side in an instant, her expression filled with concern. "Kaelen, are you okay?"

Kaelen nodded, though his voice was weak. "I'm… I'm fine. We did it."

Alyssa smiled, though it was tinged with weariness. "We got the relic. That's what matters."

As they celebrated their victory, the temple began to tremble, the walls shaking as the ancient magic that had held it together began to unravel. The collapse of the guardian had triggered a chain reaction, and the temple was starting to fall apart around them.

"We need to get out of here!" Kaelen shouted, forcing himself to his feet.

Alyssa didn't need to be told twice. Together, they sprinted toward the exit, the temple collapsing behind them, stones falling and the ground cracking beneath their feet. The path they had taken to reach the chamber was now a gauntlet of collapsing debris and crumbling walls, but they pushed on, driven by the need to escape before the entire structure came down on top of them.

The exit was in sight, the massive stone doors still open, but the temple was falling faster now, the ceiling cracking and the walls crumbling into dust. With one final burst of speed, Kaelen and Alyssa dove through the doors, landing hard on the ground outside as the temple collapsed in a deafening roar of stone and dust.

For a moment, they lay there, catching their breath, the relic clutched tightly in Kaelen's hand. The storm had returned, the rain pounding down on them as if the very heavens were trying to wash away the remnants of the battle they had just fought.

Kaelen rolled onto his back, staring up at the dark clouds overhead, the sound of the collapsing temple still ringing in his ears. They had won, but it didn't feel like a victory. The guardian was gone, and they had the relic, but the cost had been high, and the Shadow Keeper's influence was growing stronger with every passing moment.

Alyssa sat up beside him, her eyes scanning the ruins of the temple. "We made it out," she said, her voice quiet but steady. "This isn't over, is it?"

Kaelen shook his head, the weight of the relic heavy in his hand. "No. This is just the beginning."

They had the relic, but the journey was far from over. The Shadow Keeper was still out there, and the battle for the Nexus Crystal was only just beginning.

With a final look at the ruins of the temple, Kaelen and Alyssa rose to their feet, their determination renewed. The road ahead was uncertain, and the challenges were greater than ever, but they knew what they had to do.

Together, they would face whatever came next, no matter the cost.

Chapter 18

The storm's fury had only grown since they escaped the collapsing temple, its howling winds and driving rain making the journey through the treacherous landscape even more perilous. Kaelen and Alyssa pressed forward, each step a struggle against the elements and the weight of the relic they had fought so hard to obtain. The Nexus Crystal fragment, now safely tucked away in Kaelen's pack, pulsed with a subtle energy that seemed to resonate with the storm itself, as if both were connected by the same dark force.

The landscape was unforgiving—steep cliffs rose on either side, their jagged edges silhouetted against the roiling sky.

The path ahead was narrow and slick with rain, and each step felt like a battle to stay upright. The storm made it nearly impossible to see more than a few feet ahead, and the constant rumble of thunder echoed ominously through the mountains.

"We need to find shelter," Kaelen shouted over the din, his voice barely audible above the roar of the wind. "We can't keep going like this."

Alyssa nodded in agreement; her face set in a determined expression as she scanned the area for any sign of cover. The rain had soaked them both to the bone, and the cold was beginning to seep into their very bones. They had been moving for hours since the temple's collapse, but the storm showed no signs of letting up, and the environment was becoming more hostile with each passing moment.

"There!" Alyssa pointed to a small cave nestled in the side of the mountain, its entrance partially obscured by overgrown vegetation. It wasn't much, but it would provide some respite from the relentless storm.

They made their way toward the cave, the ground treacherous beneath their feet. Kaelen nearly slipped several times, his exhaustion making it harder to keep his balance. But with Alyssa's help, they managed to reach the cave, stumbling inside and collapsing against the rough stone walls.

The cave was small but dry, its entrance offering just enough shelter to keep out the worst of the storm. Kaelen dropped his pack to the ground and leaned back, closing his eyes as he tried to catch his breath. The sound of the rain pounding against the rocks outside was deafening, but at least they were out of the worst of it.

"We need to regroup," Alyssa said, her voice quiet but steady. "We've been pushing ourselves too hard. We need to think about our next move."

Kaelen opened his eyes and looked at her, nodding in agreement. "We have the relic, but the Shadow Keeper's power is growing. We've seen what he can do to the timeline—the storm, the temporal distortions… it's all him."

Alyssa frowned; her gaze distant as she considered their situation. "We can't let him get his hands on the Nexus Crystal. If he does, he'll be unstoppable."

Kaelen reached into his pack and pulled out the relic, holding it up so they could both see it. The fragment of the Nexus Crystal glowed faintly, its light pulsing in time with the storm outside. It was a small piece, but the power it contained was immense—enough to shift the balance in their favor, if they could figure out how to use it.

"This is our only advantage right now," Kaelen said, his voice filled with a mix of determination and uncertainty. "But we don't know how to use it, and we don't know how much time we have before the Shadow Keeper finds us."

Alyssa stared at the relic, her expression hardening with resolve. "We need to find a place where we can use it against him. Somewhere with enough temporal energy to amplify its power. The problem is, we don't know where that is."

Kaelen nodded, feeling the weight of their situation pressing down on him. The relic was powerful, but it wasn't enough on its own. They needed to find the Nexus Crystal, the true source of the power that had shaped their world for so long. Time was running out, and the Shadow Keeper's influence was spreading faster than they could counter it.

"We've seen the signs," Kaelen said, his mind racing as he tried to piece together their next steps. "The temporal distortions, the unnatural phenomena… they're all signs that the timeline is starting to break down. The Shadow Keeper is using his power to destabilize it, to weaken the barriers that protect it."

Alyssa's eyes met his, a grim understanding passing between them. "He's trying to force us into making a mistake. To rush in without thinking, or to retreat and give him more time. Either way, he wins."

Kaelen clenched his fists, the frustration and fear building inside him. "We can't let him manipulate us. We have to stay ahead of him, to find a way to use the relic before he does."

Alyssa nodded, but her expression was conflicted. "Where? Every moment we spend searching is another moment he's gaining more control. We need to make a decision, and soon."

As if in response to her words, the air in the cave suddenly grew colder, the light from the relic flickering as a sense of dread settled over them. Kaelen and Alyssa exchanged a wary glance, both of them instinctively reaching for their weapons.

Before they could react, the entrance to the cave was filled with a dark, swirling mist, and from within it, a figure began to emerge. The mist coalesced into a humanoid shape, its form shrouded in shadows that seemed to writhe and shift of their own accord. The temperature in the cave plummeted, and the very air seemed to crackle with dark energy.

Kaelen felt his heart skip a beat as he recognized the presence—there was no mistaking it. The Shadow Keeper had found them.

The figure stepped forward, the shadows peeling away to reveal a tall, imposing man clad in dark, tattered robes. His face was partially obscured by a hood, but Kaelen could see the faint glint of eyes that burned with an unnatural light. The Shadow Keeper's presence was overwhelming, a force of darkness and despair that seemed to seep into the very walls of the cave.

"So, you've finally come this far," the Shadow Keeper said, his voice a low, resonant growl that sent chills down Kaelen's spine. "You're too late. The timeline is already mine."

Kaelen and Alyssa rose to their feet, their weapons drawn, but the Shadow Keeper made no move to attack. Instead, he simply stood there, his gaze fixed on the relic in Kaelen's hand.

"You've done well to survive this long," the Shadow Keeper continued, his tone almost mocking. "You cannot hope to stop what is already in motion. The Nexus Crystal will be mine, and with it, I will reshape the timeline as I see fit."

Kaelen felt a surge of anger and fear, but he forced himself to remain calm. "We won't let you destroy everything we've fought for. The timeline doesn't belong to you."

The Shadow Keeper's lips curled into a cruel smile. "Doesn't it? After all, it was your actions that led us here, Kaelen. Your choices, your failures... they are what have brought the timeline to the brink of collapse."

Kaelen's grip on the relic tightened, the weight of the Shadow Keeper's words pressing down on him. He knew that the Shadow Keeper was trying to manipulate him, to sow doubt and despair. The truth was, some part of him feared that the Shadow Keeper was right—that his actions had indeed set them on this path.

"Enough!" Alyssa's voice cut through the darkness, sharp and defiant. She stepped forward, her weapon raised. "We're not afraid of you. We've fought your minions, we've faced your traps, and we've come out stronger. We're not going to let you win."

The Shadow Keeper's smile faded, replaced by a cold, calculating expression. "Bold words, but they will not save you.

The timeline is unraveling, and soon, there will be nothing left for you to protect."

With a sudden burst of speed, the Shadow Keeper lunged forward, his hand outstretched toward Kaelen. Kaelen was ready—he raised the relic, channeling its power through the gauntlet, creating a barrier of light that deflected the Shadow Keeper's attack.

The impact sent shockwaves through the cave, the walls trembling as the two forces clashed. The Shadow Keeper recoiled, his eyes narrowing in anger as he realized the power of the relic.

"So, you've learned to wield it," the Shadow Keeper said, his voice filled with a dangerous edge. "Do you truly understand its power? Or are you simply a fool, playing with forces you cannot control?"

Kaelen didn't respond, focusing all his energy on maintaining the barrier. The relic's power was immense, but it was also draining—he could feel the strain it was putting on him, the energy seeping away with each passing second.

Alyssa moved to Kaelen's side; her weapon ready as she prepared to defend him. The Shadow Keeper's presence was overwhelming, but she refused to back down. They had come too far to give in now.

For a moment, the three of them stood in a tense standoff, the air crackling with energy as the storm raged outside. The Shadow Keeper's eyes flicked between Kaelen and Alyssa, as if calculating his next move.

Then, with a sudden burst of dark energy, the Shadow Keeper unleashed a wave of force that shattered Kaelen's barrier, sending him and Alyssa crashing against the cave walls. The impact knocked the wind out of Kaelen, his vision blurring as pain shot through his body.

The relic slipped from his grasp, clattering to the ground as the Shadow Keeper advanced on them. Kaelen struggled to rise, but his body refused to obey, the exhaustion and pain too much to overcome.

Alyssa was quicker, pushing herself to her feet and placing herself between Kaelen and the Shadow Keeper. Her eyes blazed with determination as she raised her weapon, ready to fight to the last breath.

The Shadow Keeper simply laughed, a low, mocking sound that echoed through the cave. "You think you can stand against me? You are nothing but a fleeting moment, a speck of dust in the flow of time. I am the master of the timeline, and you... you are nothing."

Alyssa didn't flinch, her grip on her weapon steady. "Maybe we're nothing to you. We won't stop fighting. Not now, not ever."

The Shadow Keeper's expression darkened, and he raised his hand, dark energy swirling around his fingers as he prepared to strike. Before he could unleash the attack, something unexpected happened.

The relic, lying forgotten on the ground, began to pulse with light, growing brighter and brighter until it filled the entire cave with a blinding radiance. The Shadow Keeper recoiled, his form flickering as the light washed over him, the darkness that surrounded him retreating in the face of the relic's power.

Kaelen felt a surge of energy as the light enveloped him, banishing the pain and exhaustion that had gripped him. He pushed himself to his feet, the gauntlet on his arm glowing in response to the relic's power.

With a roar of defiance, Kaelen reached out, channeling the relic's energy through the gauntlet and directing it toward the

Shadow Keeper. The light intensified, becoming a beam of pure energy that struck the Shadow Keeper head-on, driving him back with a force that shook the entire cave.

The Shadow Keeper let out a furious scream as the light consumed him, his form dissolving into shadows that were swept away by the relentless power of the relic. The cave trembled violently, the walls cracking as the storm outside reached a deafening crescendo.

And then, with a final burst of light, the Shadow Keeper was gone, his presence erased from the cave. The storm outside began to die down, the wind and rain subsiding as the darkness lifted.

Kaelen collapsed to his knees, the relic falling to the ground as the light faded. He was exhausted, every muscle in his body screaming in protest, but the relief of their victory washed over him like a cool wave.

Alyssa was at his side in an instant, her expression a mix of concern and disbelief. "Kaelen... you did it."

Kaelen shook his head, struggling to find his voice. "No... we did it. Together."

Alyssa smiled, her eyes shining with a mixture of pride and exhaustion. "We're not done yet, though. The Shadow Keeper... he'll be back."

Kaelen nodded, his gaze drifting to the relic, which now lay dormant on the cave floor. "You're right. This was just the beginning. We need to find the Nexus Crystal... before it's too late."

The realization hung heavy in the air, the weight of their mission settling over them once more. The Shadow Keeper had been driven back, but his threat was far from over. The timeline was still at risk, and the final battle was yet to come.

For now, they had survived. They had faced the Shadow Keeper and lived to fight another day. And as they looked out at the now-calm sky, the storm finally dissipating, they knew that they would continue to fight, no matter the cost. Because the timeline—past, present, and future—depended on it.

Chapter 19

The morning after the storm dawned bleak and gray, the sky a murky blanket of clouds that obscured the sun. Kaelen and Alyssa moved with purpose, but the weight of the previous day's events lingered heavily on their shoulders. They had barely escaped the Shadow Keeper's grasp, and the urgency of their mission had never felt more pressing.

Kaelen's mind was still reeling from their encounter with the Shadow Keeper. The relic had proven powerful, but it had also been clear that it wasn't enough to defeat him. They needed more—more information, more allies, and, most importantly, the

Nexus Crystal. Without it, their chances of stopping the Shadow Keeper were slim.

They had found a small, sheltered glade to rest in for the night, but sleep had been elusive. The air was thick with tension, as if the world itself was holding its breath, waiting for the next blow to fall. The storm had finally passed, leaving behind a landscape that felt eerily calm, almost as if it was the eye of a larger, more dangerous storm yet to come.

Kaelen packed up their meager belongings, his movements efficient but strained. His body ached from the battle, and the exhaustion that had set in was bone deep. There was no time to dwell on that now. The Shadow Keeper was still out there, and they needed to move quickly.

"We need to figure out our next move," Kaelen said, breaking the silence that had settled between them. "The Shadow Keeper isn't going to wait for us to catch our breath."

Alyssa nodded, her expression as resolute as ever. "We can't do this alone. We need help—people who can stand with us when we face him again."

Kaelen couldn't argue with that. The Shadow Keeper had already proven that his power far surpassed theirs. They needed allies, and they needed them quickly. "Do you have any ideas where we can find them?"

Alyssa thought for a moment, her brow furrowed in concentration. "There's a place… an old sanctuary. It's said that some of the Time Keepers who survived the fall retreated there, hiding from the Shadow Keeper's influence. If they're still there, they might be willing to help us."

Kaelen's heart quickened at the prospect. "Where is it?"

Alyssa hesitated, glancing around as if the very trees might be listening. "It's not far from here, deep in the forest. But it's hidden—protected by powerful wards that keep it off the map. We'll have to find it the old-fashioned way."

Kaelen nodded, his determination hardening into resolve. "Then we go. If there's a chance we can find allies there, it's worth the risk."

They set off immediately, moving quickly through the forest, the tension between them now a driving force. The forest was dense, the trees towering above them and creating a canopy that cast long shadows on the forest floor. The ground was uneven, covered in roots and undergrowth that made their progress slow, but they pushed on, driven by the urgency of their mission.

As they walked, Kaelen couldn't shake the feeling that they were being watched. The forest seemed to press in around them, the silence almost unnatural. Every crack of a branch or rustle of leaves set his nerves on edge, and he found himself constantly glancing over his shoulder.

Alyssa must have sensed it too, because she tightened her grip on her weapon, her eyes scanning the forest with a wary intensity. "We're not alone," she said quietly, her voice barely above a whisper.

Kaelen nodded, his own hand moving to the hilt of his weapon. "We need to be careful. The Shadow Keeper's influence might be reaching further than we thought."

They continued on, their senses on high alert, but the feeling of being watched never left them. The forest grew denser the deeper they went, the trees seeming to close in around them, and the light filtering through the canopy grew dimmer, casting the forest in a perpetual twilight.

After what felt like hours of walking, they finally reached a clearing. At the center of the clearing stood a massive, ancient tree, its trunk gnarled and twisted, its branches reaching up toward the sky like skeletal fingers. The air around the tree was thick with power, a subtle hum that vibrated in the back of Kaelen's mind.

"This is it," Alyssa said, her voice filled with a mixture of awe and caution. "The sanctuary."

Kaelen stepped forward, feeling the energy pulsing through the ground beneath his feet. The tree was ancient, far older than anything else in the forest, and it radiated a sense of both strength and protection. It was clear that this place had been a refuge for many, a sanctuary hidden away from the dangers of the world.

But as they approached the tree, something strange happened. The air around them began to shimmer, the light warping and twisting until the entire clearing was filled with a soft, golden glow. Kaelen felt a sudden pressure in his chest, as if the very air was pressing down on him, and he struggled to breathe.

Alyssa reached out, her hand brushing against his arm, grounding him. "It's the wards. They're testing us."

Kaelen nodded, gritting his teeth as he pushed forward. The pressure intensified with each step, the air growing thicker and harder to move through, but he kept going, driven by the knowledge that this was their only chance to find the help they needed.

Finally, after what felt like an eternity, the pressure suddenly lifted. The air around them returned to normal, and the golden glow faded, leaving the clearing bathed in the soft light of the setting sun.

They had passed the test.

As they reached the base of the tree, the bark began to shimmer, and a doorway appeared, carved into the trunk. The door was made of the same ancient wood, intricately carved with symbols that Kaelen recognized as those of the Time Keepers.

Alyssa exchanged a glance with Kaelen, her expression one of cautious optimism. "This is it. Let's hope they're willing to help."

They pushed open the door and stepped inside. The interior of the tree was far larger than the exterior suggested, a vast chamber filled with soft, warm light. The walls were lined with shelves filled with ancient tomes and artifacts, and at the center of the room stood a group of figures, their faces hidden by the hoods of their robes.

Kaelen felt a surge of relief as he recognized the symbols on their robes—these were indeed the remnants of the Time Keepers, those who had survived the Shadow Keeper's onslaught and gone into hiding.

One of the figures stepped forward, pushing back their hood to reveal a weathered, stern face. The man's eyes were sharp, taking in Kaelen and Alyssa with a mixture of suspicion and curiosity.

"You've passed the wards," the man said, his voice deep and commanding. "Not many have done that. What brings you to our sanctuary?"

Kaelen stepped forward, holding the relic in his hand. "We need your help. The Shadow Keeper is growing stronger by the day, and we can't stop him alone. We have a fragment of the Nexus Crystal, but we need to find the rest before it's too late."

The man's eyes narrowed as he studied the relic, his expression unreadable. "The Shadow Keeper's reach is long, and his power great. Why should we risk ourselves for a battle that may already be lost?"

Alyssa's voice was steady as she responded. "Because if we don't fight, there won't be anything left to save. The timeline will be shattered, and everything we've ever known will be lost. We have to try, no matter the odds."

The man was silent for a long moment, his gaze piercing as he weighed their words. Finally, he nodded, though his expression remained grim. "Very well. We will help you, but you must understand that this will not be easy. The path to the Nexus Crystal is fraught with danger, and the Shadow Keeper will stop at nothing to prevent you from reaching it."

Kaelen nodded, feeling a renewed sense of determination. "We're ready. Whatever it takes, we'll do it."

The man turned to the others, who had remained silent during the exchange. "Prepare the sanctuary. We will need all the power we can muster if we are to face the Shadow Keeper."

The other Time Keepers moved swiftly, gathering around a large, circular platform at the center of the chamber. As they began to chant, the air in the room grew thick with energy, the very walls vibrating with the power that was being called forth.

Kaelen and Alyssa watched as the Time Keepers worked, their movements precise and purposeful. The platform began to glow with a soft, golden light, and symbols appeared on its surface, shifting and changing as the energy intensified.

"This platform will take you to the Nexus Crystal," the man explained, his voice low and serious. "But be warned—the closer you get, the more dangerous it will become. The Shadow Keeper has likely set traps, and his minions will be waiting for you."

Kaelen took a deep breath, steeling himself for the journey ahead. "We're ready."

The man nodded, stepping aside to allow Kaelen and Alyssa to approach the platform. "May the light guide you."

With that, Kaelen and Alyssa stepped onto the platform, the energy swirling around them in a dazzling display of light and power. The air crackled with anticipation, and Kaelen felt the familiar pull of the timeline as the platform activated, sending them hurtling through space and time.

The journey was disorienting, the world around them a blur of colors and shapes that seemed to stretch and twist in impossible ways. Kaelen felt the relic in his hand pulse with energy, guiding them toward their destination. Alyssa was at his side, her presence a steadying force amidst the chaos.

And then, with a sudden jolt, they arrived.

They stood at the edge of a vast chasm, the ground beneath them crumbling and unstable. The air was thick with the stench of sulfur and decay, and the sky above was dark and foreboding, filled with swirling clouds that crackled with lightning.

On the far side of the chasm, Kaelen could see it—the Nexus Crystal, glowing with a brilliant light that cut through the darkness like a beacon. Between them and the crystal stood an army of the Shadow Keeper's minions, the Legion of Shadows.

Alyssa gripped her weapon, her eyes narrowing as she assessed the situation. "This is it. The final push."

Kaelen nodded, his heart pounding in his chest. "We have to get to the crystal before the Shadow Keeper does. It's our only chance."

Without another word, they charged forward, the ground shaking beneath their feet as the Legion of Shadows advanced to meet them. The battle was fierce, the air filled with the clash of steel and the roar of dark energy as Kaelen and Alyssa fought their way through the enemy ranks.

The relic in Kaelen's hand pulsed with power, each strike imbued with the energy of the Nexus Crystal fragment. But the Legion was relentless, their numbers overwhelming, and Kaelen could feel his strength beginning to wane.

Alyssa fought beside him, her movements fluid and precise as she cut down one enemy after another. Even she was beginning to tire, the weight of the battle pressing down on them both.

As they neared the edge of the chasm, Kaelen realized that they were running out of time. The Shadow Keeper's influence was growing stronger, the air around them thick with his presence.

And then, with a sudden surge of power, the Shadow Keeper himself appeared on the far side of the chasm, his form shrouded in darkness. His eyes glowed with an eerie light as he raised his hand, sending a wave of dark energy crashing toward them.

Kaelen raised the relic, channeling its power to create a shield that deflected the attack. The force of the impact sent him and Alyssa staggering back, the ground beneath them crumbling as they struggled to maintain their footing.

"We're not going to make it!" Alyssa shouted; her voice filled with desperation.

Kaelen knew she was right. They were outnumbered, outmatched, and running out of time. He couldn't give up—not when they were so close.

With a final burst of determination, Kaelen charged forward, his eyes locked on the Nexus Crystal. The relic in his hand glowed brighter, its power surging as he called upon everything he had left.

And then, just as he reached the edge of the chasm, he made the hardest decision of his life.

He turned to Alyssa; his voice filled with a calm resolve. "You have to go. Take the relic and get to the crystal. I'll hold them off."

Alyssa's eyes widened in shock. "No! I'm not leaving you behind!"

Kaelen shook his head, his expression firm. "You have to. If we both stay, we'll lose everything. You're the only one who can finish this."

Alyssa hesitated, her heart torn between staying with him and doing what needed to be done. She knew he was right. They couldn't both survive this.

With tears in her eyes, she nodded, taking the relic from his hand. "Promise me you'll find a way back."

Kaelen forced a smile, though he knew it was a promise he might not be able to keep. "I promise."

And with that, Alyssa turned and ran, the relic in her hand guiding her toward the Nexus Crystal. Kaelen watched her go, his heart breaking with every step she took away from him.

There was no time to dwell on it. The Shadow Keeper was advancing, his dark energy swirling around him as he prepared to strike. Kaelen gripped his weapon, his resolve hardening into a fierce determination.

This was it. The final push. The last stand.

Kaelen took a deep breath, steeling himself for the battle to come. And then, with a roar of defiance, he charged forward, meeting the Shadow Keeper head-on.

The battle was brutal, the air filled with the clash of light and darkness as Kaelen fought with everything he had. Even as he fought, he knew that he was only buying time—time for Alyssa to reach the crystal, to finish what they had started.

And as the world around him began to crumble, Kaelen felt a strange sense of peace. He had done everything he could. Now, it was up to Alyssa.

The light from the Nexus Crystal grew brighter, cutting through the darkness as Alyssa reached it. Kaelen's vision blurred, the world fading away as the power of the crystal consumed everything around him.

And then, there was nothing but light.

Chapter 20

The air around the Nexus Crystal was electric, pulsing with a raw energy that crackled through the atmosphere. Alyssa could feel it in every nerve, a sensation that was both exhilarating and terrifying. The crystal hovered before her, suspended in the center of a swirling vortex of light and dark, its power unlike anything she had ever encountered. She tightened her grip on the relic, the ancient artifact glowing brighter as it resonated with the crystal's energy.

She knew that controlling the Nexus Crystal was the key to stopping the Shadow Keeper. As she stood there, so close to the source of all time, the magnitude of what she was attempting began to sink in. The crystal wasn't just an artifact—it was a living force, the very heart of time itself. And it was volatile.

As Alyssa hesitated, the ground beneath her feet began to tremble, the vibrations growing stronger with each passing second. She could feel the darkness gathering, a suffocating presence that threatened to overwhelm the light. The Shadow Keeper was closing in.

From across the battlefield, the Shadow Keeper emerged, his form a towering mass of swirling shadows, his eyes glowing with a malevolent light. His presence seemed to distort the very fabric of reality, warping time and space around him as he approached. The air crackled with dark energy, and the ground split open in jagged cracks, as if the earth itself recoiled from his power.

"You've done well to come this far," the Shadow Keeper's voice boomed, deep and resonant, echoing through the chaotic landscape. "But you're a fool if you think you can control the Nexus Crystal. Its power is beyond your comprehension."

Alyssa felt a surge of fear, but she quickly pushed it down, steeling herself for what was to come. "I don't need to control it," she called back, her voice steady despite the chaos around her. "I just need to stop you."

The Shadow Keeper laughed, a sound that sent chills down her spine. "Stop me? You can't even begin to understand what you're dealing with. The Nexus Crystal is the source of all time, all reality. And I will use it to reshape the timeline as I see fit."

Alyssa didn't respond. She knew there was no point in arguing with him. Instead, she focused on the relic in her hand, feeling its power resonate with the crystal. She needed to act, and fast, before the Shadow Keeper could wrest control of the Nexus Crystal from her.

Summoning all her courage, Alyssa raised the relic and channeled its power toward the Nexus Crystal. The energy from the relic surged into the crystal, causing it to glow even brighter. For a moment, it felt like the entire world was holding its breath.

And then, the battle truly began.

The Shadow Keeper lunged forward, dark energy swirling around him as he unleashed a torrent of power at Alyssa. She barely had time to react, raising the relic just in time to deflect the attack. The impact sent shockwaves through the battlefield, the ground shaking violently as the two forces collided.

Alyssa gritted her teeth, struggling to maintain control as the Nexus Crystal's power surged through her. It was overwhelming, the energy coursing through her body like a storm, threatening to consume her. She held on, focusing on the task at hand—keeping the Shadow Keeper at bay.

Meanwhile, across the battlefield, Kaelen was locked in a desperate struggle of his own. The Legion of Shadows swarmed around him, their dark forms twisting and shifting as they attacked from all sides. Kaelen fought with everything he had, the relic in his hand glowing with a fierce light as he struck down one enemy after another.

The odds were against him. The Legion of Shadows was vast, their numbers seemingly endless. Kaelen's strength was waning, his movements growing slower with each passing moment. He could feel the exhaustion settling into his bones, the relentless assault pushing him to his limits.

He couldn't stop. Not now. Not when Alyssa was counting on him.

The Time Keeper

With a final burst of determination, Kaelen unleashed a wave of energy from the relic, pushing back the Legion of Shadows long enough to catch his breath. He glanced toward the Nexus Crystal, where Alyssa was still battling the Shadow Keeper, and his heart clenched with fear. She was in danger, and there was nothing he could do to help her.

Alyssa, meanwhile, was facing a terrible choice. The Nexus Crystal's power was immense, and she could feel it responding to her will, but it was also dangerously unstable. She knew that if she unleashed its full potential, she could destroy the Shadow Keeper—but at what cost? The timeline itself could be shattered, reality unraveling in the wake of such a powerful release of energy.

The Shadow Keeper wasn't giving her a choice. His attacks were growing more ferocious, the dark energy he wielded threatening to overwhelm her defenses. Alyssa knew she had to act, and quickly.

With a deep breath, Alyssa made her decision. She wouldn't unleash the full power of the Nexus Crystal—not yet. Instead, she would try to weaken the Shadow Keeper, using just enough of the crystal's energy to push him back without risking total destruction.

She focused on the relic, channeling its power through the Nexus Crystal in a controlled burst of energy. The crystal glowed with an intense light, and for a moment, it seemed to burn away the darkness that surrounded the battlefield. The Shadow Keeper recoiled, his form flickering as the light seared through him.

He wasn't defeated. Not yet.

The Shadow Keeper let out a roar of fury, his form shifting and expanding as he gathered his remaining strength for a final attack. The ground beneath him cracked and splintered, the air filled with the sound of shattering reality as time itself began to warp around him.

Realizing that he was on the verge of being overpowered, the Shadow Keeper made a desperate decision. He couldn't win this battle, not here, not now. He could still ensure that his defeat would come at a heavy cost.

With a final, defiant surge of power, the Shadow Keeper turned his attention away from Alyssa and toward the Veil of Reality itself. He unleashed a torrent of dark energy, directing it at the very fabric of time. The Veil began to tear, the seams of reality unraveling as the Shadow Keeper's power ripped through it.

"No!" Alyssa screamed, realizing what he was doing. She tried to stop him, but it was too late. The damage was done.

The Veil of Reality, the barrier that protected the timeline from corruption, began to weaken, its once-solid structure now fragile and fraying at the edges. Time itself started to behave unpredictably, with moments looping, stretching, and collapsing in on themselves. The battlefield was thrown into chaos, the very laws of nature bending and breaking under the strain.

The Shadow Keeper, his form flickering and unstable, let out a final, mocking laugh. "You may have won this battle," he snarled, his voice echoing through the fractured reality. "The war is far from over. The timeline is mine to command, and you cannot stop what is coming."

And with that, the Shadow Keeper vanished, his dark form dissolving into the shadows as he retreated into the depths of time.

Alyssa collapsed to her knees, the weight of the battle finally catching up with her. She had driven him back, but at a terrible cost. The Veil of Reality was weakened, and the timeline was now more vulnerable than ever. She could already see the effects of the damage, the world around her flickering and shifting as time lost its stability.

Kaelen staggered over to her, his body battered and bruised, but his eyes filled with concern. "Alyssa... are you okay?"

Alyssa looked up at him, her expression filled with a mixture of exhaustion and determination. "He's gone... but the Veil... it's broken."

Kaelen glanced around at the chaotic landscape, the realization of what had happened sinking in. "We have to fix it. We have to find a way to repair the Veil before it's too late."

Alyssa nodded, struggling to her feet with Kaelen's help. "But how? The Nexus Crystal... it's too powerful. I don't know if we can control it."

Kaelen squeezed her hand, his voice steady despite the uncertainty that lay ahead. "We'll figure it out. We've come this far—we can't give up now."

Together, they stood before the Nexus Crystal, its light still glowing softly, though it was now tinged with a faint darkness from the Shadow Keeper's influence.

As they prepared to leave the battlefield, Kaelen and Alyssa knew that their journey was far from over. They had to find a way to repair the Veil, to restore the timeline, and to stop The Shadow Keeper before he could do even more damage.

The future was uncertain, the road ahead filled with challenges they couldn't yet imagine. They had each other, and together, they would face the dangers ahead.

Epilogue

The Shadow Keeper's retreat through the torn fabric of time was a journey that mirrored his current state—fractured and weakened. The energy that had once surged through him like a tempest now sputtered, barely enough to maintain his form. He had fled, not in triumph, but in desperation, escaping the battlefield that Kaelen and Alyssa had turned against him.

The portal to his lair—a hidden place beyond the reach of ordinary time—opened before him, a swirling vortex of darkness that beckoned him back to safety. As he stepped through, the disorienting whirl of colors and shattered moments faded, giving way to the cold, dimly lit chamber that served as his sanctuary.

The chamber was a vast, echoing space, its walls lined with remnants of forgotten timelines, fragments of worlds that no longer existed.

The Shadow Keeper stumbled, his steps unsteady, and his form flickered, the edges of his body dissolving into shadow before reforming again. He was barely holding himself together, the battle having drained him of most of his strength. he had survived, and that was all that mattered.

As he approached the center of the chamber, a large, circular platform began to glow faintly, activated by his presence. Above it, a shimmering portal began to form, swirling with dark energy. The portal pulsed with a cold, menacing light, a gateway that connected him to the one being he served—the one he feared as much as he respected.

Chronus.

The portal stabilized, and from within it, a figure began to materialize. Chronus appeared, his form tall and imposing, cloaked in shadows that obscured most of his features. Only his eyes were clearly visible—two cold, glowing orbs that radiated power and control. The very air around him seemed to bend to his will, the dark energy crackling with latent fury.

The Shadow Keeper knelt before the portal, his head bowed low in respect and fear. "Master," he rasped, his voice strained and hollow. "I have returned."

Chronus's gaze bore into him, assessing, calculating. "You were defeated," he stated, his voice devoid of emotion, a simple acknowledgment of fact.

The Shadow Keeper flinched but forced himself to speak. "I underestimated them, Master. The new Time Keepers—Kaelen and Alyssa—possess the relic and a fragment of the Nexus Crystal. They were stronger than I anticipated."

Chronus remained silent for a long moment, his gaze unyielding. The Shadow Keeper felt the weight of that silence pressing down on him, a cold dread settling in his core.

"They weakened me," the Shadow Keeper continued, desperation creeping into his voice. "But I did not leave without striking a blow of my own. I weakened the Veil of Reality, tearing at its very fabric. The timeline is destabilizing as we speak. Time itself is beginning to unravel."

At this, Chronus seemed to consider, his eyes narrowing slightly. "And yet, the Nexus Crystal remains out of my reach," he said, his voice low and dangerous. "Two Time Keepers stand in my way. This outcome is... disappointing."

The Shadow Keeper lowered his head even further, his form trembling with fear. "I will not fail you again, Master. I will gather more power, recover from this defeat, and when the time is right, I will strike them down. The timeline will be yours to command."

Chronus's gaze remained fixed on him, unreadable. The Shadow Keeper could feel his master's power, a cold, merciless force that seemed to see through him, stripping away his defenses and leaving him exposed.

Finally, Chronus spoke, his voice carrying a quiet menace. "The Veil may be weakened, but it is not enough. The timeline must be brought to its knees, and the Nexus Crystal must be mine. You will do whatever is necessary to ensure this outcome."

The Shadow Keeper nodded eagerly, relief flooding through him as Chronus's words offered a chance for redemption. "It will be done, Master. I will not rest until the Nexus Crystal is yours."

Chronus turned slightly, as if considering something beyond the portal, his expression thoughtful. "Remember, Shadow Keeper," he said, his voice a low rumble that reverberated through the chamber. "I created you for a purpose. Fail me again, and there will be consequences."

The Shadow Keeper's form flickered with fear, his voice barely above a whisper. "I understand, Master. I will not fail."

Chronus said nothing more. His form began to dissolve into the swirling darkness of the portal, his presence fading but leaving behind a lingering sense of cold, unyielding power. The portal closed with a final, ominous flash, plunging the chamber back into dim silence.

The Shadow Keeper remained kneeling for a moment longer, his head bowed as he gathered his thoughts. He had survived, but just barely. And now, the weight of Chronus's expectations pressed down on him, a constant reminder of the consequences of failure.

He rose slowly, his form still flickering with instability, and moved to a darkened alcove at the edge of the chamber. Here, within a hidden recess, he drew forth a crystal orb, its surface swirling with dark energy. Within its depths, he could see fragments of the timeline, images of Kaelen and Alyssa as they fought to repair the damage he had inflicted.

His eyes narrowed as he watched them, the orb reflecting his deep hatred and resentment. They had won this battle, but the war was far from over. He would recover, grow stronger, and when the time was right, he would strike again.

For now, he would bide his time. The Veil of Reality was weakened, the timeline vulnerable. It was only a matter of time before it collapsed entirely, and when that happened, Chronus would be ready to seize control.

And as for Kaelen and Alyssa, the new Time Keepers who dared to challenge him—they would learn the true meaning of despair. The Shadow Keeper would ensure it.

He returned the orb to its alcove, a cold smile twisting his features as he retreated deeper into his lair. The future was uncertain, the timeline in chaos, but one thing was clear:

The Shadow Keeper would rise again, and next time, there would be no escape for those who opposed him.

Made in United States
Troutdale, OR
12/21/2024

27132943R00184